BETWEEN THE LINES

A COLLECTION OF SHORT STORIES

VARDAAN PANDEY

INDIA • SINGAPORE • MALAYSIA

Notion Press Media Pvt Ltd

No. 50, Chettiyar Agaram Main Road,
Vanagaram, Chennai, Tamil Nadu – 600 095

First Published by Notion Press 2021
Copyright © Vardaan Pandey 2021
All Rights Reserved.

ISBN 978-1-68523-402-7

This book has been published with all efforts taken to make the material error-free after the consent of the author. However, the author and the publisher do not assume and hereby disclaim any liability to any party for any loss, damage, or disruption caused by errors or omissions, whether such errors or omissions result from negligence, accident, or any other cause.

While every effort has been made to avoid any mistake or omission, this publication is being sold on the condition and understanding that neither the author nor the publishers or printers would be liable in any manner to any person by reason of any mistake or omission in this publication or for any action taken or omitted to be taken or advice rendered or accepted on the basis of this work. For any defect in printing or binding the publishers will be liable only to replace the defective copy by another copy of this work then available.

CONTENTS

Prologue *5*

1. Acquaintances 7
2. 10 Weeks Later 29
3. The Apple 45
4. The World's Best Chicken 56
5. Family Dinners 67
6. Sasha 80
7. Hostages 103

Cover Designed by Rashika Singhal

PROLOGUE

I began writing this book sometime in 2020, when a certain virus arrived in our lives and just turned everything upside down. A lot of my feelings from that period made their way into some of the short stories; the fact that I was unable to meet my friends, the fact that I was stuck at home all day, every day, the fact that the future looked bleak, and the fact that I was spending 20 out of 24 hours in front of my laptop, or my phone, or the TV. I was saved from tha by the support of my friends, family and teachers. I felt inspired. So much so that I wrote a whole book.

The title refers to the name of a writing workshop I attended in July 2020, and also to the multiple layers you might find in my stories. During the workshop, I met some of the most interesting people from across the world, people my age, with whom I spent one of the best two weeks of my life. Some of the stories in this book stem from ideas that I had and developed during this workshop, and would like thank the facilitators and students involved.

I would like to thank my parents, who 'motivated' me to keep writing this book, who were after my case until I did something conclusive, even if it meant stopping me from binging all 9 seasons of the office. Their unwavering support and constant encouragement provided a huge boost to my confidence during a testing time, and this book would be nothing without their support. Thanks to my sister as well, the enforcer of my parents' will.

I would like to thank my friends and classmates, whom I've met over the course of the last 6 years, ever since I changed schools. A lot of my writing was influenced by the relationships I shared with some of my friends and classmates, and during the pandemic, a lot of you were there to provide support, some of you even giving feedback on the early drafts of this book and helping make it what it is now.

A big thanks to my editor, yana, for her feedback and determination in helping out a newbie like me.

And to you, the reader, I wish a magnificent reading journey ahead.

Peace among Worlds.

Thank you,

Vardaan Pandey.

ACQUAINTANCES

The jet-black Mercedes sputtered to a halt at the side of the highway. Cars zoomed past while its driver fumbled with a pack of cigarettes in his hand. Finally managing to extract one, the driver lit it up, took a long drag on it, and exhaled, surrounding himself with smoke for a few moments. His spiky blonde hair, which was all over the place, was slowly gathering a large amount of sweat, which was also trickling down his cheeks and settling on his tuxedo, but he refused to turn on the air conditioner, owing to the limited amount of fuel in his car. The driver was scowling. His right fist was clenched on top of the seat and he was smoking through gritted teeth, which were leaving marks on the body of the cigarette with every drag he took. His blue eyes stared straight ahead, taking in the views of the long road as cars hurtled past, without giving him even a little bit of consideration. None of the cars stopped to see whether he was doing all right. Nobody stopped to enquire why he had stopped at the side of the road on a blistering hot day and this made Marshall clench his fist even tighter.

Marshall Carter was an actor. That was how he introduced himself to anybody and everybody he met.

The actual truth was that he had not appeared in front of the camera in the last 7 years and his last acting venture had been a disastrous stage production of The Shining, which had also been his theatrical directorial debut.

Marshall had catapulted to success many moons ago as a 22-year-old in the short-lived sitcom *Acquaintances*, a show about six acquaintances in their twenties who get in touch and become close friends. The show garnered critical acclaim and extremely high ratings, but when *F.R.I.E.N.D.S.* arrived in 1994 on a rival network and eclipsed the success of *Acquaintances* overnight, the creators were left with no choice but to pull the show off air. The show did go on for long enough to immortalize Carter's role as the charming and slightly antagonistic James. He became known for his quick wit and comedic timing, and many of his phrases became ingrained in the language of the youth subcultures of that period. Following the cancellation of Acquaintances, Carter branched out into films and enjoyed a period of success until the mid-2000's, following which his career tanked. A series of box-office failures coupled with his growing alcoholism, unsuccessful rehab stints and other legal disputes made him infamous amongst his peers. Roles which would normally be served to him on a silver platter were being offered to him after longer intervals and he became a staple of many cash cow YouTube channels' Top 10 lists like: "Top 10 Actors who fell out of fame." He usually ranked near the top of these lists, which indicated that he had been a great star, bordering on god level, but had suffered a rather substantial decline in fame in recent years. Apart from very brief cameos and extremely rare guest appearances, there was nothing left for Marshall to do.

Unlike many of his contemporaries, Marshall was not timeless. Which was largely his own doing. Actors like my man Clint Eastwood, who have 50-60-year long careers usually keep their body in excellent physical condition, limiting the amount of substances they consume, and ensuring that their body is ready to meet the demands every role requires. Marshall was unable to do that. Marshall had peaked within a span of 15 years, and his continuous substance abuse and inability to fix the direction of his life had landed him in an extremely worrisome situation. He lacked the commitment to get himself back in shape, in order to save his career in some way, and that only made him feel worse about himself.

The break from the silver screen led to Marshall experimenting with theatre, which, as stated, had been disastrous. His creative output was overshadowed by the rap sheet he'd built for himself, with intoxication-related offences being the most common.

After unsuccessfully meddling with theatre, Marshall had embarked on the current phase of his life. The "businessman" phase. This phase was also not bearing any fruit of his labour and his failure on this front was sealed when he drunkenly revealed his plan to market a 3-in-1 haircare product that would revolutionize the haircare industry, to none other than the sales representative of a haircare products company, which was not faring very well.

Sure enough, this company had soon released a product similar to what had been described by Marshall, and had regained its status as a pioneer in the field of haircare products. The representative had been promoted to Vice President and Marshall's drinking had escalated to new levels.

He was nearing 50 now, and he was no longer the handsome, happy and charming man that America had fallen in love with, before Chandler Bing. His previous outgoing, social animal persona had now been replaced with a much more reserved and morose human being, who was constantly going through an existential crisis. He'd also lost out on his once chiselled body, which was now dealing with an extra 20 kilograms that it really did not require. His tall frame and dress sense did prevent him from looking adversely fat whenever he was in public, but every time he looked at himself in the mirror, he stared at himself in disgust.

Marshall's continued failure in all fronts of life had led to him experiencing his worst existential crisis ever, and his gloom was further compounded when he received the tragic news of Ted Eriksen's death.

Marshall and Ted had been best friends since before the popularity of the internet. They had shared many memorable experiences since childhood and used to refer to each other as brothers. They had been in the same class since primary school, had gone to the same college and when Marshall went to Hollywood, Ted followed him, acting as his agent. It was Ted who was instrumental in brokering the deals that led Marshall to his stint at the top. Soon enough, after Marshall had reached the pinnacle of his career, he became egotistical and treated Ted poorly, ostracizing him and even having an affair with his long-time girlfriend, which he attributed to his alcohol abuse and inability to think straight. Their relationship soured and the two drifted apart. Marshall sank into a downward spiral, while Ted set up his own management company and talent agency, becoming the manager of several top athletes, whilst also establishing a scouting network which helped him in signing some of the brightest young talent to his agency and he in turn gave them the opportunity to receive lucrative contract offers from some of the biggest teams in the country. Ted also branched out into film production and had easily and very promptly eclipsed Marshall's success, both financially and professionally. Although he had managed to carve out a successful career for himself, Ted was still plagued by the after-effects of Marshall's actions and like his former best friend, had begun abusing substances to deal with his personal struggles, often having wild parties with his clientele. Like Marshall, Ted also gained a significant amount of weight, and like Marshall, he made no efforts towards reducing it, losing out on his boyish charm and instead looking like a stereotypical business executive, whose clothes were always too tight.

It was only after a court-mandated rehab stint shortly before his death, that Ted finally became clean and decided to go on the path of recovery and become sober. Becoming sober also made Ted realize that he did not want to have any regrets about his life and decided to get back in touch with his former best friend. But before he could lay down the foundation of contacting Marshall, he had a heart attack in his sleep and never regained consciousness.

Marshall had wept when he read the message from Ted's mom.

"The Eriksen family invites you to the funeral of their beloved Ted, who ascended towards his heavenly abode this week. In accordance with family tradition, the funeral will be held on the grounds of the Eriksen estate, followed by a memorial service.

In grief and remembrance, Nancy Eriksen."

The message was followed by the address of the estate and a link to access the location on Google Maps. A further message stated that, as Ted's long-time friend, Marshall had been requested to be present as a pallbearer and to give a eulogy at the funeral.

He had continued to cry for many hours after reading the message and his meltdown had culminated in his picking up the nearest object (a bottle of whiskey) and smashing it on the floor.

There had been so much tension between them, for such a long time. It led to Marshall debating with himself whether or not he should go. He wanted closure, he wanted to finally settle the matter. A part of him wanted to apologize but was reminded of things Ted had said all those years ago, when their friendship had collapsed. Would a call to the grieving mother suffice? After more weeping and debating, he ended up calling Ted's mother, with the intention of firmly declining the invitation, but the pain in her voice made him alter his resolve. Left with little to no choice, he told Nancy he would be there. And so, on a perfect Sunday morning on the day of the funeral, Marshall found himself awake 3 hours before his usual waking-up time. He shaved his beard for the first time in 6 months, cleaned the hair out of his nose and ears, combed his hair into his favoured style, went through a major moisturization routine and was now looking a little bit like his former self.

He wore his best tuxedo, which was a little too tight for him and went out without drinking his usual 4 glasses of whiskey in the morning.

He got into his Mercedes, which started with a loud groan and began his voyage.

When you have a funeral that is far away, and a straight highway, the mind subconsciously slips into a contemplative mode. A long, straight road with nothing really happening and you start to think, "What the hell am I doing?", "Where am I in life?" You question your own existence and your place in the circle of life and the whole grand scheme of things. Marshall's mind was entering this existential phase, when he was jolted back to reality by the realization that he'd been squeezed to the side of the road by a speeding, blood-red Chevrolet.

Marshall hurled abuse after the car and accelerated to draw level with the Chevy. It was occupied by a group of very beautiful girls, barely over 21, all of whom were dressed as though they were going to the beach or had had their clothes stolen. There was no beach in the city. The nearest was a five hour drive away.

"What do you think you're doing?" Marshall yelled towards the car. He honked, tried to get their attention, even tried some over-the-top distracting tactics, but to no avail. The cars were racing each other, as if they were in *Fast and Furious* and, weaving through traffic, Marshall spewed the usual invective while manoeuvring past an 89-year-old lady trying to make an exit in her 33-year-old vehicle. Eventually, he lost sight of the Chevy, and cursing, found himself on the side of the road, sweating profusely inside his car due to the sweltering heat and cursing merrily. He was angry that his top-of-the-line Mercedes (though lacking seven years' worth of service), had been outrun by a Chevrolet, being driven by a female. He was not particularly concerned that a Chevrolet had outrun him. He liked the brand. He was angry that a bunch of arrogant girls had enough courage to almost run him off the road, defeat him in a race, and not even apologize to him for putting his life in danger. He was angry at everything. He sat seething on the side of the road for a solid few minutes. He finished the cigarette, tossed the stub outside the window and contemplated a bit more before finally deciding that getting angrier would not be prudent and that he should continue with his journey.

Marshall arrived at the service, being held at the large estate of Ted's family on the outskirts of the city. It was a grand old red brick mansion, plucked right out of an Agatha Christie novel. It had been Eriksen family property for over 100 years now. It spanned 15 acres of land, with the main house containing 10 bedrooms, 2 formal dining rooms, and a central lounge which was the main venue for any event the family would host. The property also had some guest houses, detached from the main house, which were used in the event of the main house not being able to accommodate everyone. There was also a servant's lodge, which housed the family housekeeper. The rest of the property was surrounded with lush greens.

At the very edge of the property, was the Eriksen's own private cemetery, where many generations of the family had found their final resting spot.

The grandeur of this house would put Marshall's modest 3-bedroom apartment to shame.

Marshall bumped two cars and finally parked in one and a half parking spots. He looked at himself in the mirror once again, and sprayed on a fresh coat of perfume, before exiting the car, and entering the home.

The house was packed with people. And all kinds of people. In a corner, Marshall could see some of Ted's clients from the sports industry, discussing a recent game of basketball and lamenting Ted's death, claiming that he would have been proud of the way one of his latest recruits had played. In another corner, members from the film industry were discussing Ted's latest film, *The Legend of Serpent Hill,* a film Marshall had heard about, but had never gotten around to watching it. The film had broken several box-office records, and one of the members of the group exclaimed that it deserved to win all the awards it had been nominated for. Moving forward from there, Marshall met some grieving family members, who were telling each other how nice a man Ted had been. Marshall skulked around, giving half-baked greetings to people. Some recognized him, others didn't. He continued moving until he reached the main attraction. The champagne tower and the snack counter.

Avoiding a distraught relative, he grabbed a glass of champagne and proceeded to meet with the grieving mother, who was standing close by. Nancy Eriksen with her thin bony face, blue eyes and white blond hair, slightly resembling Jane Fonda, was interacting with other guests, collecting their blessings and ushering them along towards the funeral service. She looked stronger than Marshall had expected her to be. Inside she was broken like Mr. Glass's bones, but from the outside she looked like the toughest woman you'd ever meet.

She smiled when she saw Marshall, showcasing all 32 pure white pearls. Marshall returned the smile, albeit with slightly more yellow teeth.

"Hi, Marshall, I'm so glad you were able to make it."

"Anything for Ted. How're you holding up?"

"Not good."

"Yeah, I figured. Anything I can do to support you guys?"

"Not necessarily. There's some work we have to do, but we have it all planned out. No help needed. But anyway, it's good to see you, Marshall. Where have you been? I haven't heard from you in years."

"Yeah, I got busy. Did a few plays on Broadway. Currently, I've been working to establish myself in the start-up industry. I tried to market this business idea that revolves around rentals."

"Oh, like car rentals?"

"No, lifestyle essentials. You rent your shampoo, or your nail cutter, you don't have to buy it, just rent it."

"That doesn't make any sense."

"I know it doesn't. In my head I was making millions but when I was laughed out by 7 different corporations, I realized how much trouble I was in."

Nancy chuckled, and they both hugged.

"Come on, the service is starting shortly. Let's get you a seat."

Marshall followed Nancy into the gardens, which had been readied for the service, which was taking place on a portion of land close to the cemetery. The coffin had been placed on a catafalque, and chairs had been set up in rows of 5, facing the coffin. Next to the coffin was a small podium, intended for the priest and for the guests delivering their eulogies. A framed photograph of Ted, taken before his dark period, showcasing his lovely smile, his curly black hair and his charming green eyes, was placed next to the coffin as well. Nancy assigned Marshall to a seat in the second row, designated for close friends, and Marshall found himself seated next to one of Ted's producer friends, who introduced himself to Marshall as Barney Robinson. He was an excitable fellow, 10 years Marshall's junior, and claimed to be a big fan of his work, stating that Marshall's performance on Acquaintances had been one of the best he had ever seen. The two struck up a conversation about their respective relationship with Ted, which was dissipated by the arrival of the priest.

The priest made his way to the podium, Bible in hand. He was dressed in a cassock. His black hair was combed to the side, allowing his round face to appear very prominent. His brown eyes stared at the bereaved from behind thick, round glasses. He uttered some prayers from the bible, said Amen twenty-two times, and then requested Ted's mother to deliver her eulogy.

One by one, Ted's immediate family and extremely close friends stepped up and delivered their eulogies.

The final eulogy was to be delivered by Marshall, who had been listening intently to the words of everyone before him. He stepped up to the podium, took out the sheet of paper which contained his ramblings, and began speaking.

"I knew Ted for 28 years. There wasn't a thing we did not do together.

"I can't fully comprehend that he's gone. It seems as though it was yesterday when we were talking on the phone and I can't believe the fact that when I call his number from now on, it will go unanswered and won't be picked up by my best friend.

"Ted and I drifted apart over 15 years ago. I made some terrible decisions. I wronged Ted. He made many sacrifices for me and in return I only gave him grief. He was a very kind and loving soul, who did not deserve the negativity that I sent his way. I will regret the fact that I did not apologize to him, that I did not mend my ways. That I refused to give him the closure he deserved. I will forever regret it. Despite our problems, I still consider Ted to be my best friend, and I hope he's found his peace, and I hope he can forgive me. Rest easy, Ted. Thank you.

Marshall stepped aside, making way for the priest to give some concluding remarks and then to request the pallbearers to carry the coffin to the burial site. Marshall, alongside 5 other men, carried the casket and placed it in the trench which bore Ted's name on the gravestone. He took a long look at Ted's grave, before apologizing to him and leaving, allowing the gardener to begin shovelling dirt into the grave.

Back inside the house, Marshall was deep into a conversation with Barney in the central lounge, who as it turned out, had also acted as a producer on *The Legend of Serpent Hill*, and had a wide variety of films in the pipeline which he was now pitching to Marshall.

"I know you haven't acted in some time, but I think you should really consider *Serpent Hill 2.* We're on the hunt for a new villain and this could be the perfect comeback role for you. You could reinvent your career, and we could give your character a backstory based on your own life. The audience would be able to sympathize with you, and this can help in changing their opinion about you."

"Why are you doing this, Barney?" Marshall asked, with a hint of a smile playing across his face.

"I think you're a good actor. The reason I became your fan is because of your skill. I know for a fact that there is a lot of talent buried inside you, and maybe I can help you make a comeback. Don't you want to make a comeback?"

"That's the point. I don't really know what I want to do. Even if I say I want to return, there's still a lot of things I'll have to take care of. Losing all this weight is probably on top of the agenda, because nobody would want to see me like this. I certainly wouldn't. And you're right. I haven't acted in a long time. I'm rusty. Most actors do 2 films a year. I haven't done one in 7, and all I had to do in that film was act scared and scream. I'm wary of picking something like this."

"Marshall, I know it's a big ask. It would take a lot of convincing to a lot of people to finally get you on board. But I just happen to be one of the biggest guys in the industry right now. My voice has authority. I *can* get people on board. I'll tell you this, Marshall. Scripting starts a few weeks from now. It'll probably take 3-4 months to finish it. If you can show me that you are committed to this role, and that you are ready to make a comeback, I can do your bidding and convince people to give you a shot. Just give me the evidence to back up my claims, and I can get this job done for you.

Look at Robert Downey Jr, look at Winona Ryder. Their career had problems. They had long breaks. Look at how brilliantly they rebounded. Don't think too little of yourself. If you have the belief and have the desire, I can help get you back on top."

Barney's words were getting through to Marshall. He had managed to give Marshall a desire that was long lost. He made the fire in his belly burn again.

"You know what, Barney. I think I will give it a shot."

"That's great news, Marshall. I have a meeting with the other producers today. I can start negotiating with them now, if you like."

"That would be amazing."

"Great."

"Can you tell me a bit more about the actors? Who do I have to fight against?"

"Well, as far as I know, Chalamet, who's the main guy, is returning. None of the others have confirmed yet. I did come here with another actress who I think would do well, but I seem to have lost her in the crowd."

"Yeah? What's her name?"

"Sabrina Taylor."

The smile on Marshall's face disappeared.

"Oh wait, there she is. Sabrina, look who I found."

Marshall turned around to find himself face to face with a person he thought he would never see again.

Back in the day, Marshall had decided to write, direct and act in a stage adaptation of *The Shining*, without any prior theatrical experience, and stating that it would be the first true horror play. He had managed to get backing for it somehow, and claimed that this production would give a more comprehensive portrayal of what it was like to live in the Overlook Hotel and be Jack Torrance. If by that he meant that he would go crazy, then he was right. He was neck-deep in production, and did not get along with any of his cast members, having frequent arguments with them. The previews were disastrous and everybody who watched it claimed it was terrible. Everyone, except Sabrina. Marshall had started dating her shortly after he began working on the production. She was this really beautiful, salt of the earth lady, with shimmering brown hair that came down to her shoulders, hazel eyes that you could get lost in, and looks that could drive you wild. She worked as a waitress at a local coffee shop and was an aspiring actress. Marshall had promised her that she had a great career ahead of her and that he would cast her in his next play. She attended every rehearsal and was full of praise for a production that was slowly tanking due to terrible reviews from critics and audiences alike.

After a particularly disastrous performance, which included the female lead forgetting her lines and running offstage and the prop master accidentally destroying props worth twenty thousand bucks, a furious Marshall lambasted every member of the cast and crew before chucking Danny Torrance's tricycle towards the kid who played the role.

As he left the theatre, he found Sabrina standing in the rain with a ring in her hand.

Usually, a man does that kind of stuff. She went down on one knee.

"Look, Marshall, I know we have only been dating for three months, but I feel that we have a bond that you see in romantic comedies. I want to settle down with you, and have kids with you, and live the rest of my life with you. Will you marry me, Marshall?"

Marshall, already seething, was patently oblivious to the tenderness of the moment and just stared at her for a full minute while she gazed back, unnerved but tense. Then, with a shrug, he stepped around the kneeling Sabrina, knocking her over onto the wet sidewalk, and muttered, "It's over, girl."

He got into his car and played rap music loudly to drown out the shower of garbled expletives emanating from the weeping Sabrina and drove off.

It had taken Sabrina months of therapy to recover, but memories of Marshall still haunted her. She went on to make a name for herself in theatre, and was now engaged to a successful businessman. Barney had liked her interpretation of Linda Loman on Broadway, and had approached her with an opportunity to take her career to the silver screen, an offer she accepted. And so, she found herself at Ted Eriksen's funeral, a man she did not know, when she encountered a man she did know, and one she hated very strongly.

"Hey, Sabrina, did you get your breasts enhanced? You look good."

"Shut up, just shut up. How dare you come here? How dare you show me your face after what you did? Do you have any idea what I went through that night? After you left me, do you have any idea how much pain you caused me?"

"I'm sorry, Sabrina, I really am."

"You horrible, horrible man. You don't care for anybody who cares about you. You are just a sick individual. I went inside and I saw what you did to your cast. Everybody was crying. Everybody was disappointed. And you. You just used all of them, you used me, and then left us all alone and broken."

Barney turned to look at Marshall.

"Again, Sabrina, I'm really sorry. I was not myself that night. I overreacted and I am really sorry about what I did to you and to everyone."

"You could have at least called me and apologized. I waited, and I waited and I waited and I waited and I waited for you to call or come back. But you didn't."

"I–"

The high-pitched haranguing had attracted attention, and a crowd had formed around the couple. Nancy was trying to separate the two, as was Barney, who was trying to calm Sabrina down in an effort to prevent the altercation from becoming very intense, which was proving to be futile. The topic had now escalated from his walking away to his many infidelities and allegations of abuse and harassment. Sabrina was dishing out charge after charge of how Marshall had treated her during their relationship.

Marshall, trying to put a foot in the argument, asked Sabrina: "Why haven't you moved on then?"

That was the final straw.

"You're just a pathetic man. You can't do anything right. You couldn't make TV shows, you could not make films and the only play you ever produced was worse than *The Last Airbender*. You've just wriggled your way towards an inch of fame and famous friends and are now just taking advantage. Do you have a single iota of talent? No. You're just a less attractive and talentless Matthew Perry."

Marshall had no response to this. People around him had fallen silent. Sabrina was breathing heavily. Her eyes had become full of tears, which was prompting mascara tears to run down her cheeks, significantly altering the way she looked.

"Can we talk in private, Sabrina?"

"Ok."

Marshall and Sabrina left the lounge, leaving many people surprised and shocked about what had transpired. Eventually, the crowd dispersed and resumed their conversations and the housekeeper began clearing the glass shards on the floor.

Inside a room just past the lounge, Marshall and Sabrina had begun talking.

"Do you have anything left to say, Marshall?"

"No. Sabrina, I'm sorry I wronged you. I've done a lot of terrible things to a lot of kind people and you were one of them. If you heard what I said about Ted, I really meant it. You didn't deserve this treatment from my side. You might think that this is fake, but it is not. Ted's death has really opened my eyes and made me realize that my behaviour was wrong. All I can do now is to make you believe that I am a changed person. I don't want to die 15 years from now, with only a few movies, failure and regret to my name. I have been given a major opportunity to change my fortunes, and I am going to take it. I am going to change who I am. If you can find it within you to understand this and to forgive me, I would appreciate that. If you want to continue hating me, you can. Whatever gives you closure. I hope that the next time we meet, our interaction is a lot more positive."

Marshall's words stunned Sabrina. He exited the room, and entered the lounge, where he apologized to everybody who had to witness the ruckus. He said a final few words to Barney, took a business card from him, bade goodbye to Nancy, and left the house.

As he got into his Mercedes, his demeanour was slightly more positive than it had been that morning.

With something to look forward to, Marshall started his car and sped back towards his home.

10 WEEKS LATER

(This story is a dialogue between Francis and Alice, who are a separated couple currently on the way to the hospital to meet their 17-year-old daughter, Megan. Francis, dressed in a blue polo shirt and black jeans, is a 40-year-old advertiser whilst Alice, dressed in a black dress with white polka dots, is also 40, and is a freelance writer, who is unemployed 300 out of 365 days every year. Their daughter is a high school student and a very good basketball player, being the captain of her varsity team and attracting the attention of scouts from some of the biggest colleges in the country.

At present, our couple is waiting at a red light and a discussion transpires.)

F: How did she get into the hospital in the first place?

A: She came home all fine, but then started experiencing a stomach ache, like, two hours ago. I gave her a pill, which should have worked, but she still had it. So, I asked Jonathan to take her, and I called you over.

F: What was Jonathan doing at your house?

A: He was over for, you know, drinks and stuff, and for a chat.

F: Drinks, huh? We might be separated but we're still legally married. I'm still your husband. You can't mess around with other men until you decide you want a divorce or not.

A: REALLY? Who are you, talking about faithfulness, huh? The man with the golden gun? You've slept with more women than Bruce Wayne, and you're talking to me about staying faithful?

> (*Faithfulness to a partner is a particularly touchy subject, ever since Alice walked in on Francis involved with a friend of hers, which subsequently led to the discovery of Francis's multiple infidelities.*)

F: You've got it wrong.

A: Oh, I have? Enlighten me. Have all my best friends, who've said they slept with you, got it wrong? They slept with a lookalike, huh? Someone with the exact same features as you, exact same looks as you? You say you were faithful to me. You, the pious man, the man with the chastity belt, who has never put a foot out of line. That's who you are, right?

F: It wasn't like that. You see...

A: See what? What do you want me to see? How are you going to twist the story further? Just admit to the fact that you were unfaithful, that you were the cause of our marriage being the shitshow it was, that you were unhappy with your life at home and you used your charming looks to get with a lot of women to ease your unhappiness. But no, even though the evidence is in front of you, you refuse to just give me the closure I need. You refuse to admit that you were wrong. You continue to lie, continue to twist the story. Can't you just say that you were at fault, for once?

(Stunned silence.)

F: Can this wait? If I wanted to get chewed out, I would've arranged a coffee date, not this. We have a priority right now.

A: Oh, yeah, yeah. It can wait. Everything can wait. You are the king of the world, aren't you? Your priorities, your girlfriends, your work. What about me? Did you ever think about my priorities? My desires, my needs? "Hey Alice, I am getting a transfer, so you have to quit your extremely high paying job, OK? Thank you." I put everything on the line, just so you could have the career you wanted. And this is how you repay me. By not letting me have a say in anything?

(It's funny. They never fought before marriage. Everyone always believed they would be one of those Hallmark couples. Married for 50+ years. But they proved the world wrong. In a bad way.

Alice and Francis had been together since school. It was a given, considering the fact they were the two most popular and best-looking students in the entire school. Francis, a lanky, 6-foot guy, with sharp facial features, blue eyes and the most charming smile ever. And Alice. What could one say about Alice. She looked as though the gods had sculpted her and given her the best features any woman could have the benefit of receiving. She had silky black hair surrounding her round face, with piercing green eyes that had the ability to draw you in.

It did not come as a surprise to anyone when Francis finally asked her out during their middle school graduation, and she accepted.

They wed shortly after graduating from college, which marked a turning point in their lives.

Three months after their wedding, Alice got pregnant. The pregnancy exacerbated her underlying mood swings and anger issues, later diagnosed as bipolar disorder, and led to the first set of arguments amongst the couple, regarding the two options to deal with the pregnancy. Alice, heavily against abortion, refused to go through with the procedure, despite Francis's numerous claims regarding the impact a child would have on them, that they were not ready to be parents. Alice refused to consider his arguments. Now parents to a daughter, our young couple stayed together and fought. Steadily, cracks began to appear in their marriage. Alice began resorting to substances to cope with her bipolar disorder, and resisted Francis's numerous attempts to help her get clean. Francis, long disillusioned with life at home, began seeking solace outside and after a time, their relationship was non-existent and they stayed together solely for the well-being of Megan.)

F: Why does everything have to be about you? Why do you take everything I say straight to the heart, without a second thought? I made mistakes in my life, I'm sorry for some, not sorry for others. What else can I do? You made your choices, I made mine. We are where we are. Can you shut it for once and let me focus on the road, please?

A: Fine. I'll shut up.

F: Thank you.

(The smooth voice of John Mayer floods the speaker system of the car, as the warring couple falls silent. They pull up into the hospital parking lot and walk in, while Alice resists Francis's attempt to hold hands with her. They take the lift to the third floor. As they emerge, Jonathan, who is standing nearby, comes over

to give Alice a hug. Jonathan is a handsome, 28-year-old business executive. He is wearing a T-shirt with a picture of the band Nirvana on the front, and a pair of dark blue jeans.

Alice had met him at a singles' night at one of the local bars six months earlier, shortly after the separation. They have since been on eighteen dates and are discussing the possibility of moving in together. The hug is followed by a tense and curt handshake between the two men.)

J: She's in Room 303, doing fine.

F: Thanks.

A: I appreciate the support, Jon. Would you like to come inside with us?

J: I'm not allowed inside right now. Hospital policy. Only parents are allowed. See you later, though.

(The parents step inside Room 303. Megan, all of seventeen, is lying on the bed, dressed in the hospital gown, watching a made-for-TV romantic comedy. Megan is almost a carbon copy of Alice, with almost the same physical features, the only difference being her smile, which is something her father says he gifted to her. She showcases this smile as her parents walk in.)

F: Hi, Meg! How are you doing?

M: I'm okay. Definitely feeling better.

F: How is the pain now?

M: It comes and it goes. The doctors did some scans on me, and said they'll get the reports in some time.

F: Do you have any idea how this could have happened? Did you hurt yourself, eat something bad?

M: I guess it's a sports related injury. Bruised myself pretty bad playing basketball today. Could be an after effect of that.

A: Could be, yeah. How long did the doctor say the results would take?

M: He said it could take an hour. He should be back soon.

(The parents continue to have a conversation with Megan, and about 15 minutes later, a doctor walks in. The badge on his coat reveals his name to be Dr Kidman. He is around 50, shorter than everyone in the room, with a slight paunch and a balding head, looking a bit like George Costanza from Seinfeld. He has a bunch of files labelled with Megan's name and addresses the parents with an air of foreboding in his voice.)

Dr. K: Hello, I assume you are Megan's parents?

A: Yes.

Dr. K: Well, Mr and Mrs Peterson, there is no way I can sugar-coat this.

A *(Shrieking)*: Oh, no! What is it, doctor? Is she going to die?

F: Let the man speak.

Dr. K: Thank you. There is nothing to worry about, ma'am. No diseases. Your daughter is pregnant, that's all.

F, A and M: WHAT?

Dr K: Our early scans detected that there was nothing wrong in the stomach. Nor were there any problems with the pancreas or liver, which may have contributed to the stomach ache. Megan mentioned she had missed a period so we got an ultrasound done, just as a precautionary measure. It reveals that your daughter is 10 weeks pregnant, which explains the sudden stomach ache

(Francis slumps into a chair, his head in his hands, struggling to deal with the situation. Alice pounces on Megan and begins an interrogation.)

Dr K: I would recommend you guys find out who the father is and bring him into the loop. It's important that you know whether he wants in or not, if your daughter plans to raise the baby.

A: What do you mean, if? Of course, she will raise the kid.

Dr K: It's important that she make the final decision, ma'am, whether she wants to have the baby or not. We are a pro-choice hospital with excellent facilities. If she wants to let go of the child, our highly trained specialists will conduct the procedure. I assure you, it would be painless.

F: Just a second, doctor. I need to know something from Megan.

Dr. K: Go ahead.

F: Can you give us the room for a minute?

Dr. K: Sure

(He steps out of the room. Alice and Francis launch into an interrogation of Megan.)

F: Who's the father?

A: If you abort the kid, I disown you.

F: Who is it?

A: No more tuition fees and no roof over your head, Megan. You can't abort the kid.

F: Who did you bone, Meg? Tell me and tell me NOW!

M: OK! I'll tell you. Calm down, please.

(Alice start a speech against abortion but Francis shuts her up. She sits down and picks up a glass of water, taking sips.)

F: It will be alright. We'll understand.

(A long pause.)

M: It was Jonathan.

(Alice spits out the water she is drinking and turns to stare at Megan, shocked.)

F: Jonathan? Her toy-boy? You're telling me you've been impregnated by the same man your mom is messing around with?

A: But how? Surely you may have had relations with someone else?

M: No.

(Francis throws his hands in the air and lets out a sigh.)
(To Alice)

F: What sort of household are you running, huh? You can't even control your own "boyfriend". Why don't you go outside and tell him he's dead meat? Tell him to run far away, because if I see him again, he has had it.

A: I want the full story. This is...a shocking revelation.

M: Please don't hurt Jonathan, he's done nothing wrong.

F: I'll decide that. Now tell me what happened.

M: Well... I came home from school and he was in the kitchen, waiting. Mom wasn't home, he said she had gone for a wine tasting and he didn't want to be drunk at three in the afternoon.

(Francis throws a disgusted glance towards Alice.)

M: My boyfriend had just broken up with me and I was very sad. Jonathan realized something was up and asked me what it was. He was really nice, he said some comforting things, and we had a nice talk. And then...it just escalated.

A: Did you use protection?

M: Of course, we did. We used a condom.

F: Did you check the expiry of the condom? It may have broken or something.

M: I didn't. It was just lying there, so we used it.

(Francis takes a seat again.)

A: So how are we going to raise the kid, Meg? You know you can't abort it.

F: It's her choice. Know this, Meg, whatever you choose to do, I will support you. And if you need a place to stay, considering your mother cannot stop drinking, my door is always open. I've changed my habits. You'll be in good hands.

(He steps out of the room and asks Jonathan to come inside.)

A: Leave Jonathan alone.

F: I'm not going to do anything to him. Why would you think that? I'm just going to talk to him, like a man, make him set his priorities straight, and let him go.

(Jonathan knocks on the door.)

F: Come in.

(Jonathan enters. As he turns to close the door, Francis sneaks up behind him. Jonathan turns around to find himself face to face with Francis, who punches him in the face. Jonathan crashes back against the door and utters an expletive. As he gets up, Francis punches him again.)

J: What the hell did I do? Why did you break my goddamn nose?

F: You knocked up my daughter, that's what you did, *Jon*. Get away from here. Run as far as you can go, and if you ever come near my family again, I swear to God I will send you to a place where nobody will be able to find you.

J: She's pregnant? But how? That's impossible. I am so sorry, Francis, I really am.

A: The best thing for you would be to leave. I will get your stuff sent over to you in some time, if there is any that you have left behind. We'll talk later, Jonathan.

(Jonathan leaves, clutching his nose.)

A: That was not a rational way to deal with that situation. What was that about a man-to man conversation?

F: What the hell do you mean by rational? Is there anything you have done that is rational? You don't have the courage to sign the divorce papers yet you're sleeping with a man who is, what, 12 years younger than you, and he is simultaneously sleeping with your daughter. This is porn logic. It does not make an ounce of sense. You're out for wine tastings in the afternoon, you're living in an apartment your sister owns, you make no money whatsoever. You've left your kid to grow up by herself, and look what's happened. And after that you tell both of us that she cannot abort it. You ruin her life, and then you take away her choice. Pray tell, what is rational?

(The argument escalates wildly with the parents throwing foul words and insults at each other. Megan, with her eyes full of tears, desperately pleads with her parents to stop fighting. The quarrelling, coupled with the departure of the bloodied Jonathan, rouses

attention in the waiting hall outside. Someone calls a nurse, who brusquely enters the room and manages to separate Francis and Alice, who were on the verge of coming to blows. She drags them outside and plonks them in seats in the waiting area, threatening dire consequences if they resume fighting. The nurse returns to Megan, who has by now shed enough tears to irrigate a small garden. Her blood pressure has skyrocketed so the nurse calms her down and offers her a glass of water and some fresh fruit.

Outside, Francis and Alice sit quietly, feeling the salty glares directed at them. Alice turns her attention to the TV, watching Kim bully Kylie in the re-run of Keeping Up with the Kardashians. Francis flips through an issue of Sports Illustrated with Kate Upton on the cover. Then he speaks in a quiet voice.)

F: Where did we go wrong?

A: I don't know, probably somewhere between your fourth affair and my first lapse into the world of Smirnoff and Jägermeister. I think our relationship collapsed when Megan was born.

F: Do you want to take care of this situation together?

A: I am not moving in with you.

F: I'm not asking you to move in with me. I'm asking you to be in this together, for Megan. This is a life-changing situation for all of us, and if we don't keep our options open and ourselves together, we will not be able to deal with this scenario.

A: She is not getting an abortion.

F: Oh, for the love of God, Alice! She starts college next year. How is she supposed to raise a kid in the dormitory? She cannot leave it behind, because I still have twenty years to go to retirement, and you are not in a situation to take care of a new-born baby. Do you want the same thing that happened to you, happen to her? You not wanting an abortion changed our entire life, Alice. You know for a fact that we weren't ready. Your mental health was all over the place and I had just started working. You missed out on a brilliant career opportunity, and we missed out on so many experiences together. Our life could have been so much different, but it wasn't, because you did not want an abortion, Alice. For the love of god, let her choose what she wants to do. If you write the story of her life before she has even thought about what she wants to do, nobody will enjoy it, least of all her. So, please, keep an open mind.

A: *(stunned)* Okay.

F: *(emphatically)* Thank you.

(To the nurse attending to Megan)

F: Any idea when she gets discharged?

N: Hopefully in an hour. We need your signatures on a couple of documents and then you can take her home.

F: Thank you very much.

(An hour passes. They sign the documents. Megan, now all changed and slightly happier, walks out with them. The temporarily reunited family drives off towards Francis's house.)

F: You want a burger, Meg?

M: Doctor's told me not to have fried food, but I'll take a McFlurry.

F: Sure thing.

(Francis pulls into the McDonald's drive-thru and orders a McFlurry. As he is ordering, a Snapchat alert lights up his phone. A snap from a woman called Kerri. Alice stares at the message for a few seconds, before dismissing the notification and turning up the volume on the radio. Francis collects the order and hands it to Megan. They drive off into the darkness.)

John Mayer (on the radio): "Your body is a wonderland..."

THE APPLE

An urban legend has it that after Einstein died, his body was flown back to the city of Ulm, his birthplace. A proper burial, with full rites, was held at the local cemetery, and Einstein was interred with national honours.

That very night, grave robbers stole his body, armed with shovels, pickaxes and whatnot. After all, it was the era before high quality policing and Albert Einstein had been the greatest living scientist and the most intelligent man in the world.

They performed a trepanation and stole his wealth of intelligence.

The local bar had a raucous crowd the next night as the bartender was serving a drink known as Getränk der Intelligenz (The Drink of Intelligence). Several young men queued up to shell out 10 Deutsche marks for the elixir. They then went home and boasted to their wives about what they had drunk.

The next night, several ladies had a drinking contest at the bar, where a certain blue liquid was the centre of attention and discussion. And the ladies went home to their men. Something went down that night at 22 different homes throughout the city.

This legend was debunked as simply being a rumour to spread craziness amongst the people.

Einstein's body and brain were never found. The German police were baffled at the body's disappearance, because the grave looked exactly as it had after the funeral.

The drink was debunked as a money-grabbing ploy.

A garbage collector apparently found bits of human flesh in the dustbin of the bar, newly christened Das Gehirn (The Brain). This went unreported.

There was nothing to bolster this legend, to prove it was true. Not a single clue was ever found and people went about their lives as usual.

About nine months later, in January, the twenty-two women who had taken part in the drinking contest at the bar gave birth to twenty-two babies, eleven boys and eleven girls, at the Ulm General Hospital.

Many, many years later, in a time when we, the contemporary generation, live, Mr. Klaus Henrichson became the youngest-ever graduate of the Royal University of Ulm, aged 18. He went on to prove all of Newton's theories wrong, instead establishing his own laws of motion TM © and gravitation TM©, winning a Nobel Prize.

Ms. Sheila Patrick-Stofferman became the first woman to travel closest to the sun, using a self-designed spacecraft to reach within 1,000,000 km of the star. She returned with stunning photographs. She, too, was awarded a Nobel Prize.

Mr. Adam Muller prevented World War III by blowing up Russian, American and North Korean missile research centres and launch bases, while sitting in his bedroom and eating bratwurst alongside toast. He was awarded a Nobel *Peace* Prize

To name a few.

One day, these twenty-two accomplished sons and daughters of those who had consumed that drink returned to Ulm, invited to be the ground breakers of the "study of teleportation" department at the Einstein Scientific Laboratory.

One was late.

Mr. Samuel Martins was not the brightest. Sure, his parents had consumed the drink. But they had not been the brightest either. Mr. Martins had inherited the intelligence of the illustrious Mr. Einstein, but also certain traits of his not-so-illustrious parents. He was a brilliant scientist, no doubt about that. He was the first person to actually travel around the world in eighty days (seventy-nine days and twenty-two hours, to be exact), visiting sites like the Great Wall of China and Machu Picchu. His colleagues, The Elite 21, did not consider this a major achievement, compared to their godlike deeds. Ms. Patrick-Stofferman said that her pod could travel around the world in two hours. Of course, the trip would not be as detailed as Mr. Martins' had been, but frankly, anyone could do it, even Muller, who had not seen daylight or nightfall since his escapades with the missiles. Being hunted by the governments of four countries was frankly no party.

People derided Mr. Martins, calling him fake wherever he went. Those who harboured some respect for him were few. A sad reality for a part-descendant of Albert Einstein.

Martins was always the one to make an eye-catching entrance. Be it in a hot air balloon, a private jet or an underwater car. He reached the lab, ten minutes late, trying to show off his new, upgraded hot air balloon.

"Oh, look, it's Marty," exclaimed Dr. Gilda Kauffmann, Ph.D.

"Hey, Mart, how you doin'?" Mr. Joseph 'Joey' Jonsson called out.

"I'm very good."

"Did you build your own balloon?"

"Yes."

"Looks very similar to one I saw on holiday in New Zealand."

"It's original, Jonsson. Shut your mouth."

"Just chill, man. Pulling your leg."

"Nice watch, Sam. Where did you get it from?"

"Patek Philippe, limited edition. I saved their owner from a Siberian tiger. Gift from them."

"You sure?"

"Oh, very nice! Jonsson, you ought to shut the dustbin you call a mouth."

"Relax, just a joke. Can't even make a joke nowadays, it seems."

The lab where the scientists were supposed to be working was a fairly large one, state of the art, constructed two floors underground on the request of Henrichson and Muller. One's request was that 'teleportal waves' were more prominent underground. The others were that people were less prominent underground.

The lab already had most of the experiment essentials assembled. A large cylindrical vessel stood in the centre of the room, connected sleekly to the roof and floor with two iron rods of negligible thickness. This was the teleporter. A small pod was placed in a corner of the room. This was the place where an apple was to be teleported.

There was a large console next to the teleporter, larger than the ones you would find at NASA. On that console were several large, complex buttons, a keyboard, a mouse, a monitor and Siri.

Henrichson immediately sat himself at the console. Everybody got themselves chairs, and soon were seated around him. A fuming Martins took a seat towards the back.

"Right, we first need the object."

The apple found its way to Mr. Henrichson. He appraised it, took its measurements, and deemed it fit for use.

"Now we need to boot up the machine."

The console was switched on. It emitted several clicks, then a flutter of lights spread across the keys, and Siri asked, "How May I Help You?" The large monitor booted up and a software opened, lighting up the screen.

This was essentially Notepad on a Microsoft computer, but far more stylish and intuitive.

"It requires us to type in the instructions."

The pathbreaking procedure required several layers of complex formulaic work, something that just one scientist could not provide. It needed the varied input of every single brainiac present in that room

Henrichson wrote in a couple of complex equations that were absorbed by the software. The teleporter was now clicking, whirring away, much to the delight of Ms. Patrick-Stofferman, who was chuckling gleefully in the corner.

Muller then stepped up to input some formulae, followed by Ms. Patrick-Stofferman, and then Dr. Kauffman. Meanwhile, Jonsson asked Siri to get him a coffee. Soon enough, assistants where wheeling in a heavy coffee machine, suited to the needs and tastes of everyone in the room. Mr. Jonsson typed his commands for the software, then Mr. Schwartz and Mrs. Troutsson did the same. Finally, at the end of the queue, it was the turn of the dark horse, Mr. Martins.

The Elite 21 watched him, coffees in hand, as Martins walked to the console.

"Don't make it go to Berlin, Sam," Jonsson said, and laughed at his own humour.

Through gritted teeth, Samuel Martins gave the all-important instructions that would govern the speed of the apple in the teleportation experiment. It was crucial that it should not be too fast or too slow.

Klaus Henrichson took over the chair once again, double and triple checking his formulas. He invited everybody to check their formulae as well and after an hour, when all was done, the moment arrived. The apple was placed in the vessel. Henrichson gave the command for teleporting the apple. He pressed the space bar.

A flash of light emanated from the vessel, then a whirring noise.

Ms. Patrick-Stofferman chuckled wildly.

Siri started counting backwards. When the countdown reached 0, the apple vanished from the vessel.

Poof. Gone.

Everyone cheered and clapped, and hugged each other.

Mr. Henrichson wheeled his chair to the small pod in the corner of the room. He took out the apple and held it up to everybody., There was even more raucous cheering. It was as if Rafiki was presenting Simba to the whole jungle.

Then the apple was placed back in the pod. Mr. Henrichson pressed some buttons on a smaller console next to the pod and flicked a switch. This console would copy the code from the larger one, and then repeat it in order to send the apple back to the main vessel.

Siri started counting once again. Henrichson wheeled himself back to the console to view this stage of the experiment. When Siri reached 0, the apple reappeared.

Half of it was missing.

It was as if someone had taken a gargantuan bite out of it.

"Was zum–?" Henrichson exclaimed, thunder-struck.

"Teleportation anomaly, Klaus. You must have flicked the wrong switch, pressed the wrong buttons," Mr. Norbert Bachmann exclaimed.

Henrichson held up a hand to silence Bachmann. He noticed a piece of paper that had certainly not been there initially. He picked it up and read it aloud:

"Thank you, Mr. Klaus Henrichson and all others. The apple was delicious. Slightly waxy but nonetheless tasty. Your experiment was quite a success, I must say, but not completely successful. Why don't you send some other delicacy next time? Maybe some roast chicken, maybe some beer. The pleasure was all mine. See you again, soon. MS."

Henrichson collapsed, mumbling incoherently. Everybody crowded around him. Dr. Kauffman checked his pulse, whilst Muller re-read the note, exclaiming incredulously. Ms. Patrick-Stofferman's hysteria slowly peaked as Henrichson continued to be unresponsive.

Suddenly, the technicians working on the ground floor were startled and alarmed by a screech that can only be described as the death wail of a banshee.

The limited edition Patek Phillipe emitted a tiny beep on his wrist as Samuel Martins hummed *Für Elise* under his breath. The apple had truly been delicious, although slightly waxy.

Mr. Klaus Henrichson was declared dead three hours later. The cause of death was deemed to be shock amounting to heart failure, accelerated by years of drinking and smoking.

At the funeral, the police questioned everyone who had been present in the lab during that fateful experiment, including Mr. Samuel Martins, but got no answers to the relatively few questions they had.

Reportedly, Klaus Henrichson's last words were: "Dear God, not again."

A few days later, the owner of Das Gehirn was arrested, for allegedly paying robbers two thousand euros to break into a local cemetery and steal the brains of Mr. Klaus Henrichson.

Ms. Sheila Patrick-Stofferman, long-rumoured love interest of Mr. Henrichson, called the act 'terrible' and 'inhuman'.

Police investigated Mr. Samuel Martins, the man who went around the world in eighty days. He had been known to have a longstanding rivalry with the deceased that had stemmed from Mr. Henrichson humiliating Mr. Martins at a public gathering to benefit the construction of a rocket that could travel to Pluto, carrying humans. Mr. Martins was detained and his house searched, but nothing suspicious was found.

Mr Martins grew to rank fourth on the Forbes list of "Richest People Alive" after he invented a watch that could make the user move at half the speed of light. The SpeedWatch TM © sold more than two million editions. Surprisingly, he never returned to Ulm after receiving a Nobel Prize and instead spent his last years in the lovely city of Interlaken. He died peacefully, aged 95, more successful than any of the other twenty-one had ever been.

No one knows who MS was and what Klaus Henrichson meant when he uttered his last words.

And, sadly, they may never know.

THE WORLD'S BEST CHICKEN

Ram was trying to impress the parents of Sita, his fiancée. He had invited them over for dinner, in an attempt to finalise the marriage and was now busy preparing the World's Best Chicken (as claimed by the recipe book and the smiling Italian guy on the cover page).

"Do Italians know how to make chicken? I thought they just made pizza."

His fiancée's parents, Mr and Mrs Chandra, did not hold him in high esteem, ever since he had accidentally spilled an entire bottle of whisky on his prospective father-in-law at a dinner party a few months earlier. They also did not appreciate the fact that he was a vegetarian and often spoke to him in a condescending manner because of this, whilst making jokes behind his back.

Ram was deeply religious, and was vegetarian for related reasons. His father hailed from the deep end of Varanasi while his mother was originally from Agra. Both his parents worked in the IT industry.

Unsurprisingly enough, the in-laws-to-be were also not on good terms with his parents for similar reasons. Mr Chandra had made the innocent "mistake" of ordering a chicken tikka when both sets of parents had gone out for dinner together. Ram's father ended up reciting the entire Hanuman prayer at the dinner table, which made the entirety of the conversation thereafter very awkward. Mr Chandra had kept his cool then but when he had returned home and downed a couple of glasses of whiskey, he had flown into a rage about the so-called vegetarians holding the country back while also describing paneer as the poor man's meat substitute. In the midst of all this, some anti-Indira Gandhi sentiments had seeped in, making it a highly politicised discussion on whether vegetarianism should be banned.

It was true Mr Chandra did not like to eat vegetarian food. He thoroughly disliked vegetarian food and the idea of people consuming it. He was a man of principle in that he did not follow any principles his father, a semi-wealthy businessman, had taught him. Mr Chandra ate a wide variety of foods, but none of them ever consisted of purely vegetarian preparations, apart from breakfast meals wherein he begrudgingly accepted the presence of porridge and cereal. Hence the outburst following the debacle of the dinner date. His wife was a tolerant and docile woman, just like her mother had been, and would accept anything her husband would say. Their daughter, on the other hand, was a rebellious child and refused to abide by the rules put in place by her parents about being agreeable and eating non-vegetarian food. She couldn't publicly disobey her father, because there was a 99.9 percent chance that he would skin her alive when they got back home and hence whenever she went out with her friends, she ordered vegetarian food. All the time.

Ram knew very well of his would-be father-in-law's disdain for vegetarian food and had hence gone about ensuring that he would serve a chicken dish of the highest quality that would lead to his prospective father-in-law becoming his actual father-in-law. But the recipe, which he obtained from a friend, turned out to be something rather bizarre.

"How to prepare the World's Best Chicken: A recipe by Lorenzo Padelli."

"Don't fight the chicken. In order to prepare a great chicken dish, you must establish a relationship with your chicken, a friendly one. The best chicken dish is one that is prepared with a chicken that you kill not long before you start preparing your dish, between 30 minutes and one hour. Any sooner or later and it will lose its taste. Bow to your chicken. The chicken should bow back. The chicken must feel as if it is the king, and you are its servant. It is also important that you prevent your chicken from getting bored. If your chicken gets bored, it will start wondering whether it came first or the egg. You have to prevent the chicken from having an existential dilemma in your kitchen, because then it will not taste as good. Within

10 minutes of bowing to your chicken, you should euthanise it. Birds do have brains, even if they aren't as advanced as us. They may not drive a car, but they can kill. And believe you me, if they get bored, they will want to kill. If you follow these instructions, your chicken will taste like heaven. It will seem as though God's angels sent a chicken from heaven to your kitchen."

And this was just the foreword.

Ram was in half a mind to throw the book away and Google the recipe when he spotted the reviews this recipe had received. Stunned to see that some of the greatest chefs in the world had praised it, he decided that however complicated it might turn out to be, he would go ahead. Anything for Sita.

Before he actually purchased the chicken, Ram had undertaken a very comprehensive ritual. He took a half-day off from work, citing personal commitments, and then went about doing tasks that would earn him karma points in God's perception. If he did a bunch of good things, the blessings would overpower the damnation. He took a proper shower and chanted the Gayatri Mantra 300 times during it. After that, he said his evening prayers at three in the afternoon. Before leaving for the butchers to purchase the chicken, he covered the eyes of every single deity in his prayer room. He then bought a chicken from the town butcher, Laxman Tiwari, brought it home and placed it in his kitchen, as he hurried around, gathering ingredients. As had been instructed, he had bowed to the chicken, and it had bowed back to him. He took out various spices from the cupboard and arranged them on the counter. It was 5.30 pm on a lovely Tuesday evening. His 'in-laws' would be arriving at 7.30. He turned to look at the chicken. The chicken looked back at him. Ram slowly approached its cage, while the bird kept its beady eye focussed on him. Tiwari had offered to get it killed painlessly, but Ram had stated that he wanted to do the honours himself.

Killing a chicken is a complicated procedure. If you want to humanely kill a chicken, then you should stun it first. For that express purpose, Ram had obtained a stun gun, for a very hefty price. You stun the chicken so that it does not feel any pain, then you practise some knife techniques in order to define the portion that you want to carve and cook. Finally, according to the recipe before you, you marinate it and fry/grill/roast/broil/bake it. Ram had prepared for the operation. His friends had asked him why he, a vegetarian, was going to cook chicken. He pointed their attention to MasterChef Canada, a cooking show where a vegetarian contestant made non-vegetarian dishes and won the competition. If she could do it, then so could he. He had watched countless YouTube videos featuring chefs and butchers on how to perfectly carve a chicken. He practised those techniques on a bottle gourd. He wanted his father-in-law to taste that chicken and, maybe, for a few good seconds, have an epiphany. An epiphany in which Ram would come riding a white stallion and tell him, "I am marrying your daughter." And the father-in-law would reply: "Yes, for sure."

All the while, the words of Lorenzo Padelli echoed in his brain. "Don't fight the chicken." "Bow to your chicken."

Progressing towards the cage, Ram took the stun gun out of his back pocket. The chicken's button eyes were fixed on his moves. It was clucking away, which is the equivalent of a human screaming. Ram advanced closer and closer, drawing the stun gun out and pressing the trigger once, experimentally, so that a nice zap of electricity illuminated the kitchen. As he leapt forward to stun the chicken, it flapped clucking out of the cage. Ram fell to the floor, hurting his nose and splattering blood all over the tiles.

Soon, chicken and human were engaged in a furious battle of wits and athleticism. The chicken was too fast for Ram, who was trying his best but unable to catch it. His attempts were proving futile, and don't even get him started on the mess that had formed from the spilled spices on the kitchen counter.

Suddenly, the chicken stopped scooting around. It went silent and motionless. Ram carefully approached it, only to find it inspecting the pool of blood that his nose had left on the floor. Ram saw his chance. Stun gun ready, he tiptoed to the chicken. As he went for the disarming move, the chicken saw his reflection in the pool of blood. It saw its life flash before its eyes and realised that it was indeed the egg that had come first. But before it could cluck out the answer to the puzzle, Ram's stun gun had done the damage. The chicken writhed on the floor, and then became still. Ram put it on the kitchen counter and cleaned up the mess in the kitchen. Satisfied with the cleanliness, he then went ahead with the slaying of the sacred bird. According to Lorenzo Padelli, a classic Italian chicken dish, prepared with chicken thighs and shit loads of olive oil among other ingredients, was the greatest chicken dish ever prepared. Ram whisked together the olive oil with some salt, pepper, rosemary, thyme, paprika and chopped basil, adding a dash of sweat to prepare the marinade. He placed the chicken thighs in the marinade and kept them there for 30 minutes before frying them. On the side, he had prepared a traditional Italian stew, which he was going to serve with the chicken. After the chicken had marinated, it was fried and baked and placed at the centre of the dining table, occupying the greatest seat. Ram even covered it with a fancy dish cover, which he had bought off Amazon. After ensuring that the chicken was perfectly positioned, Ram hurried back into the kitchen to prepare food for the vegetarians. As he heard the familiar sound of Sita's Toyota pulling into the parking space in front of his house, he was just adding the finishing touches to the Palak paneer. The doorbell rang exactly as Ram had placed the dish on his table.

Welcoming his "in-laws" into the house with a big smile, Ram offered to take his prospective father-in-law's coat. The latter obliged rather happily. Mrs Chandra complained that Ram had gotten thinner since their last meeting and asked him when he had last consumed a square meal, to which Ram responded honestly with a chuckle, "Three days ago."

He seated the family in the living room of his compact apartment and asked them whether they wanted anything to drink prior to eating dinner. The mother asked for water while the father asked for a bottle of beer, whilst making a snide remark to his wife regarding the overwhelming possibility of there being no beer, or alcohol of any kind, in the house of a religious fellow. He found himself pleasantly surprised when Ram turned up with a bottle chilled to the temperature he liked for his beer. Ram also offered them some snacks before heading back into the kitchen to prepare the final item in the buffet, garlic naan.

Just about 15 minutes later, the family and Ram were seated around the dinner table, with Mr Chandra being particularly expectant, having remarked on the delightful smells wafting in through the dining room that had hit his olfactory receptors right in the feels. Saliva was steadily building up in his mouth as Ram went about revealing all the dishes set out before finally reaching the pièce de résistance. Ram lifted the cover to reveal a chicken dish looking so delectable it would have made Gordon Ramsay wet himself with delight.

As he turned to face the family in all his glory, Ram first noticed the very familiar expression of shock on his father-in-law's face. He looked at Sita, who was looking mortified at the sight of the chicken, and then to Mrs Chandra, who was on the verge of tears.

"What is that, Ram?" Mr Chandra enquired, his voice tremulous with worry.

"This is an Italian chicken dish, claimed to be the best in the world."

"Did you not tell him, Sita?"

"I did. I sent him a text yesterday."

"What did you have to tell me?"

"Did you not read the message?"

"What message are you talking about?"

"Dad went for a medical check-up a few weeks ago. The doctors did their routine check-ups and found that he had a lump in his chest, which proved to be a benign tumour."

"What? How come you never told me about this?"

"It didn't matter at that time. The doctors associated this with his diet, as he had been eating meat almost every day of his life for the last 30-odd years. They removed the tumour and have advised him to be completely vegetarian. The message I sent you was regarding this. Did you not read it?"

"I don't really know. I have to check."

He opened WhatsApp on his phone to look for the message in question. And there it was. Monday, at 4:43 in the evening, Sita had sent a message, among a flurry of them, stating that "Dad's been advised to go on a vegetarian diet." He had not read this message, fervently occupied as he had been with the preparation of the chicken.

"Well, I guess there is only one thing left to do now," Mr Chandra exclaimed, and with that he picked up the bowl of paneer and served himself some, before passing it to his wife. Ram stared at his preparation in shock, unaware of anything around him. He did not notice his fiancée nudge him, asking him to eat. He did not observe everyone eating their food, in great silence. He did not notice his father-in-law thoroughly ingesting the Palak paneer. The same man who had wished to remove all paneer from existence was now licking his fingers after finishing his helping. Ram was still in shock when the family left.

He locked the door, and turned around to look at the chicken dish, sitting in the middle of the dining table, uneaten and cold. He stared at it for all of two minutes before picking it up and throwing it in the trash, and with it his entire hard work, blood, sweat and tears, et al., designed to make his prospective father-in-law experience nirvana. There sat the World's Best Chicken, in his dustbin, waiting for the garbage collector to come in the morning and take it away. Ram went to his room and prayed, half-laughing and half in tears, before heading off to sleep.

Life is not fair, Ram mused, drifting off into an uneasy sleep filled with dreams of his prospective father-in-law riding Ravana's chariot and telling him that he could not marry his darling daughter. It definitely obeys no set rules, he maintained, whilst squaring off with his dream vision of Mr Chandra menacing him in the battlefield of Lanka. Life is perplexing. But alas, what can one do about it? And with that thought in mind, Ram directed an arrow at his prospective father-in-law. Hit in the navel, Mr Chandra evaporated into thin air but before that he finally gave Ram permission to marry his daughter. Ram closed his eyes, rolled over onto his side and was lost in deep sleep.

FAMILY DINNERS

The dinners had soured many years ago.

This year came the denouement.

Sitting on a metal chair inside the police station, 34-year-old Jai thought about his wife, who was sweet natured and had convinced him to go to the family reunion yet again.

Was.

"Alright, Mr. Sharma, let's take this from the top. Describe to me the events leading up to the death of your wife."

Jai thought about his wife's golden skin, how, even without makeup, she would glow. He thought about her long, brown hair, which she loved to tie back in a pony tail. He thought about her deep blue eyes, which he got lost in, time and time again.

Jai hated his family. Hate, in any case, was too weak a word to describe his relationship with his family members. He did not like visiting his family members every year, just so they could see his face, comment on his life, tell him he had gained weight, then eat mediocre food, and forget about him until the next year.

"It's a long story," he managed.

Jai's father, Ajay, was a stockbroker. Having come to the States to live the American dream, he had been successful and had earned enough money to retire by the age of 40. After officially becoming a multimillionaire, Ajay Sharma moved the family to upstate New York, occupying a 16-bedroom manor at the lakeside, complete with gardener and housekeeper, something straight out of an episode of *Downton Abbey*.

There goes a popular saying, by one Mr. Michael Scott: Mo' money, Mo' problems.

And that is exactly what the Sharma's suffered from.

Problems.

With great power comes great responsibility and with greater amounts of alcohol comes a really short fuse.

Ajay Sharma had anger management issues, like his father before him. Ajay Sharma Sr. had inflicted years of physical and mental abuse on his six children, and his eldest, yours truly, had faced the brunt of these attacks. Props to Ajay Jr. that he did not turn into a madman like Ted Bundy or something, but the years he spent abusing alcohol to drown out the sorrows of his early life rendered him perpetually wobbly, alongside several underlying health issues.

He wasn't the same man physically who had come to America all those years ago. And anybody who talked about how he had grown longitudinally, he was as good as dead.

"Who else was present with you at the reunion?"

"It was just me and my family."

"So, your parents, your stepbrothers, and your sisters?"

"Yes."

"Looking at this photo, can you identify all the members of your family?"

"Sure."

Jai Sharma had a large family. His father had been married twice. With his first wife he had had two sons. Rahul and Madhav Sharma, born two years apart. After an incident which involved Ajay Sr grabbing a two-year-old Madhav by the ankle and throwing him against a wall, his first wife had separated from him and taken custody of the two kids. In later life, Ajay made amends by reaching out to them and apologizing, and building a relationship with them. The divorce did not hurt his prospects as a bridegroom though, as six months later, he was vacationing in the Bahamas with his second wife, Rajshree Sharma (formerly Tiwari), with whom he fathered four more children, including Jai, bringing the grand total of the Sharma clan to eight members.

Out of six children, there were three sons and three daughters. Rahul Sharma, the eldest, followed in his father's footsteps into the stock market, eclipsing his father's success. Unlike his father though, Rahul was a fitness freak. He had sworn off alcohol, only making room for beer, and exercised every day, without fail. Madhav Sharma was a wastrel. He'd tried his hand at multiple business ventures and had failed at all of them, and used his childhood trauma to excuse his own shortcomings. The only stroke of luck he'd had was that he married a really rich woman, who loved him for who he was.

Annika Sharma was a successful businesswoman who had set up a car rental company that had driven many out of the market with a business model that would put Tesla to shame. Nandini Sharma was a lawyer who became the youngest DA of Los Angeles and presided over many famous cases, with the most well-known being the conviction of one Mr O.J. Simpson. Mohini Sharma created her own line of beauty products, eventually putting Kylie Jenner out of business. And then there was Jai. A filmmaker.

None of the siblings had kids. Rahul was devoted to his health and his work and couldn't find time for anything else, Madhav was impotent, Annika was unmarried, Nandini was dating this guy on and off, Mohini had married a famous rapper by the name of nightpanda, but had divorced him, and his own wife had died — four months before his siblings would become aunts and uncles, and his parents' grandparents.

"Your wife was pregnant at the time of the incident, am I correct, Mr Sharma?"

"Yes, five months."

"That is sad. If you want a moment alone, I can accommodate that."

"No, it's fine. Let's continue."

The family reunion was a ploy put in place by Rajshree, who had gently suggested this to Ajay when they were both having dinner together one hot summer night. Ajay instantly agreed to the proposal, and soon the family WhatsApp group was beeping with messages.

The idea was great but to put a dysfunctional family in a room together is not a good idea. It is like telling a five-year-old kid they cannot have ice-cream. It seems like a power move, but when the kid starts screaming and begging, you question your choice. This is the same situation the Sharma's were in. You bring them all together and it seems as though they are one happy family, but when you take a look behind the curtain, you see the madness unfold.

The dinners had been going on for three years before a moment of characteristic madness brought the family to a deadly standstill. The dinner in the first year had been a relatively smooth affair. Apart from the usual drunken tirade by one of the family members, tempers had been relatively kept in check. Things started spiralling out of control the next year

onwards.

"Your sisters had a falling out."

"Yes, there was a massive argument between Mohini and Annika."

"What was the reason behind the quarrel?"

At the second dinner, the entire family had gathered in Venice for a getaway. They would have dinner by a waterfront restaurant, where they would be entertained by the beautiful locale around them. They would then stay the night in Venice, leave the next morning through Rahul's private jet (richness), and land in the Big Apple by the evening.

It was at this reunion that Jai announced that he was getting married to his partner of five years, who was not there due to work-related issues. The announcement was met with widespread appreciation. Everybody congratulated the lucky man and Rahul even offered his California estate as the wedding venue, an offer which Jai accepted.

So, all was good?

Apparently not.

The moonlight illuminated the cobbled paths of Venice, and on one of these paths walked Annika

Sharma with her sister's husband, nightpanda. The two were rumoured to have been involved before his marriage to Mohini, and the story was, in an absolute sense, true. After the arrival of the annual reunion came the arrival of what was probably the scandal of the year. The two had managed to locate a room within the 16-bedroom house and would secretly meet there to indulge in activities that could be classified as pleasure inducing. The affair had been a secret. They would meet during the night, leave in the morning, forget about it for the entirety of the year, and have the rendezvous at the next reunion.

On this moonlit night in Venice, our two cheaters were looking for an alley where they could resume their courting. Upon finding one, they had quickly gotten down to business. The thrill of it all — that is what drove these two to this act. As they grunted and sweated and scrabbled for purchase, Mohini Sharma was out on a walk with Jai. They were the closest of all the siblings and had supported each other through every moment of their lives, whether personal or professional. They were talking about nightpanda's new album, titled *Flight*, which had debuted earlier that year, and had topped the Billboard Charts for eight consecutive weeks. Jai wanted to work with nightpanda on his next film. While talking, they managed to meander in the proximity of where the lovemaking was occurring. The soft moans and the harsh grunts struck Mohini's ear, and she decided to investigate the matter and tell the couple, whoever they were, to get a room.

The sounds grew louder. Mohini reached the pair and shouted: "Get a room, guys. No coitus in public places."

Startled, the two lovers fell apart, and stared at the intruder. Mohini stared back at them, mouth open in bewilderment. Jai caught up to them and stared in horror. There was absolute silence as the four looked at one another. Mohini collapsed into the arms of Jai, and the confrontation that followed was NOT pleasant.

"I see. So, one of your sisters' husbands was sleeping with the other sister."

"That's about it. Yeah. They had a pretty violent fight back at the hotel. Everybody got involved and we had to pay the hotel twenty thousand euros when Mohini threw an antique vase at nightpanda. He left that night and now Mohini and Annika rarely talk to each other. Mohini divorced nightpanda soon after."

"The sisters did appear at the reunions though, right?"

"Yes. They are one of the prime causes of my wife's death."

The third reunion had occurred at Rahul's 28-acre vineyard estate in California, fitted out with three swimming pools and a large beachside lawn and barbeque grill, the venue of Jai's marriage, and also the site of his widowing. Mohini had been dragged to this event after Ajay threatened that he would remove her from his will. That is the level of seriousness these reunions had risen to. After the debacle in Venice, people were wary of attending this reunion, as they did not want to be drawn into the hostility that the two sisters were displaying towards each other. Luckily, Rahul's estate had 34 rooms spread over four different houses; so, it was pretty easy to hide the sisters away from each other. The only moment when tensions could flare up was during the meal.

"Your family members were worried as to how the meal would go?"

"Yes. They considered several options and ultimately decided, after speaking with both of them, that the dinner would happen as usual and an effort would be made to curb their animosity."

This was not a typical sit-down dinner. Rahul would be hosting a barbeque dinner next to the pool. The whole family was seated in chairs next to the pool, with Annika and Mohini at opposite corners. Annika had, in fact, tried to apologise for her actions, but Mohini had refused to even look at her or hear what she had to say. Rahul clinked his glass and raised a toast.

"This is for my lovely brother, Jai. Congratulations for your marriage to probably one of the best women

I have had the pleasure of knowing. And here is to the child you are going to bring into this world."

Everybody raised their glasses and drank.

Ajay got up, with an alternative toast.

"I would like to propose a toast to every single member of my family. Rajshree, my wife. Jai, Rahul, Annika, Mohini, Nandini. And, uh, Madhav. I- I'm proud of all of you."

Everybody raised their glasses and drank.

"Why did you pause before my name, dad?"

"I don't know what you are talking about, Madhav."

"You paused before my name. You said the names of the five other idiots. Then you paused before you said my name. Why did you do that, dad? Are you not proud of me?"

"Maybe I am not," said Ajay, annoyance suddenly writ on his face. He continued. "After all, you are basically living off me and your wife. You don't have a job. You are basically, in all forms, a grifter and wastrel. So, no, I'm not proud of you."

A storm was brewing on the distant horizon.

"Wow, Dad. That is really big of you, you know. You ruin my life as a child, and then you tell me you are not proud of me. Amazing. You must have balls of steel saying this to me."

"What are you insinuating? I made a mistake, which I then tried to fix. I paid so much money for your therapy. I sent you to the top psychologists in the country. All sorts of help, I gave you. If you did not respond to the treatment, how is it my fault? If you can't man up and face your problems, how is it my fault?"

"You mother–"

Rahul got up angrily.

"Madhav, I forbid you. Don't say that to dad."

"Oh yeah, big bro. What are you going to do about it, huh? Negotiate a deal? Sometimes I wish he'd thrown you against that wall instead of me."

The snowballing of this argument was taking a toll on the mood of everyone present, particularly Jai's wife, who had arisen to mediate. But one of the facts governing a dysfunctional family is that, if an argument has begun, it will be seen out till the end. So, as usual, everybody picked up their battle armour, and went to war.

"I support you, Madhav. At the very least, you have some honour, unlike Annika, who won't stop at anything to get her way, even if it means she sleeps with her sister's husband."

"Just shut up, Mohini. I have been trying to apologise to you for the longest time. I made a mistake and I am sorry."

"It's all fickle. Everything is. Your sorry doesn't mean shit to me. You ruined my marriage. There is no sorry in the world that can fix it."

"Guys, can we stop this argument, please?"

Jai and his wife had gotten into the middle of this conflict and were now desperately trying to stop people from getting into cutthroat battles. Jai was arbitrating the manly fight, while his pregnant wife was mediating between the sisters. Rajshree Sharma was sobbing quietly and Nandini Sharma had gone inside, listening to nightpanda's latest release "Existential Questions of the Broken Heart", oblivious to the drama.

As she mediated the catfight, Jai's wife felt a wave of dizziness wash over her, which startled her, and temporarily made her lose her balance. As she was experiencing this feeling, a trailing arm from one of the sisters struck her on the chest.

Jai's wife was standing on the edge of the pool. She was five months pregnant. She had never learned how to swim.

The loud splash made everybody understand the frivolity of their fight. Jai was already inside the pool, telling people to call 911. His wife had hit her head against the metal ladder. The swimming pool was slowly turning red, as was his shirt. Rahul called the ambulance, while everybody held their faces in their cupped hands.

"She died a few hours later from trauma to the head and water in her lungs. I—"

Jai began to cry. Nothing he would do would get his wife back into his arms from the jaws of death into which she had been pushed by his own family.

"Mr Sharma, how do you want to proceed from here? Will you be pressing charges against your family members?"

There was no response.

"Mr Sharma, do you need a moment?"

"They killed her. They killed my wife. Everyone in my family killed my wife, but they would have killed one another if she hadn't died first. They showed what little humanity they had left in themselves by trying to save her life, but in all honesty, none of them ever had a human heart."

With that Jai picked up the family photograph from the table and ripped it to shreds.

"None of my family was ever human," he said bitterly.

SASHA

Go! Bid the soldiers shoot.

With that line, Fortinbras bade his army give Hamlet a state funeral and drew the West End production of *Hamlet, Prince of Denmark* to a close, as the curtains fell and the audience rose in applause.

The actors joined hands backstage and as the curtain rose once again, they bowed as the swarm of cultured individuals who still valued theatre over films showered applause for the performance.

In the middle of this line of actors stood Raj Patel, a 27-year-old third generation British Indian and the man portraying Hamlet. One of the few Indian actors of note still performing onstage, Raj had had an impressive career graph and had landed a major theatre role by the time he was 20 years old. Ever since, his career had gone from strength to strength and this was the acme. Performing Shakespeare in a packed West End theatre. It didn't get any better.

The director of the play, Marshall Carter, himself a former theatre and film actor and director, of international renown, stepped forward for the applause. Following the final fall of the curtain, Marshall congratulated everybody for a brilliant performance and reserved exemplary praise for Raj.

It had been a good performance. None of the actors had forgotten their lines, the stage had been set beautifully. Everybody had acted their hearts out. Raj had even felt greater chemistry between himself and the actress playing Ophelia, who went by the name of Anne. She was new to the group, having only joined them a month earlier, but there was no doubt that she was destined to be a great actress. In the span of a month, she had established a good working relationship with everyone, and had seamlessly fit into the group as well, as if she had always been there. Something about her seemed familiar to Raj, who was in half a mind to ask her out for coffee, when his attention was taken up by some audience members requesting his autograph. Smiling, he obliged and even posed for a few photographs.

By the time these shenanigans were over with, most of the cast and crew had left, save for Marshall, who was hooking up with an audience member in the green room. Raj changed, collected his things and exited the theatre.

West End theatres can get pretty packed, outside as well. Especially for a major performance like *Hamlet*, there is always the possibility of excessive traffic, both pedestrian and vehicular. Such was the sight which greeted Raj. The streets were jammed.

Cars were sitting on the road, idling, waiting for those in front to move. The pavements were packed with milling crowds moving in multiple directions. Raj joined the mass of humanity, hoping it wouldn't take him long to reach the tube station. He was feeling pretty tired after the performance and was dreaming about a hot shower and some nice pizza when he noticed that a lady walking in front had dropped her wallet. People rushing past hadn't noticed. Raj called out after the lady, but she was already swallowed up in the crowd. The wallet, a violently red colour, had fallen on the pavement and had opened up. Raj picked it up.

It was an ordinary wallet, but more on the lines of what a man might own. It was too rugged to be a woman's and it was empty, save for some petty cash and a photograph. There was no identity of any kind. Raj had begun to shut the wallet and put it in his pocket, when his eyes landed on the photograph.

He almost dropped the wallet in shock.

It was a photo of his ex-girlfriend. Deceased ex-girlfriend. Sasha. Raj was shell-shocked to find the photograph in the wallet of a stranger. He searched the wallet again to look for some identity, but could not find any. Raj placed the photograph back in the wallet and changed direction, now heading towards the police station. He wiped sweat off his face.

All of a sudden, his mind was racing with memories of Sasha.

Their first date.

Their first hook-up.

Their first apartment, next door to where Raj used to work part-time.

Their first fight.

Their last fight.

Her funeral.

Raj hadn't shown up at the funeral. When people had enquired as to why he wasn't there, he responded with a grievous wail, asking for privacy and to mourn alone.

Sasha had passed away in a car accident a few days after telling Raj that she wanted to break up with him. They had recently had a major argument after she had walked in on him "rehearsing" with a cast member, inside their house, on their bed, with his clothes off. Raj never got the chance to explain. Sasha left before he could speak. She didn't even collect her stuff.

Raj felt guilty sometimes.

He walked into the police station close to the theatre, but had to wait, for the station was filled with people registering complaints. A lot of the complaints seemed to be about a pickpocket who was running rampant in the area. Raj, all of a sudden, felt very awkward holding somebody else's wallet in his hand, realising that the owner of the wallet could be registering a complaint regarding its loss. He took out the photograph, discreetly put the wallet in his pocket and sat down in the waiting area, hoping the crowd would peter out so that he could deposit the wallet and leave in peace.

The photograph looked brand new, as if it had been printed that very day. Sasha was looking at the camera and was smiling, wildly, showing her perfect teeth to the camera.

She looked beautiful, just like the day when he had first seen her, five years earlier.

Raj had been acting in a production of *Hamlet*, but a local one this time. He saw her in the crowd. Dead centre, in the middle row, the best seat in town, and she was smiling. She was enjoying herself. Something about her smile spurred Raj from there on and he delivered a stellar performance.

She'd asked him out later that evening, and they had a great time together, walking through the streets in the night. As people started shuffling into the nightclubs, Raj and Sasha had made out and agreed to go on another date the following week.

Soon enough, they were dating steadily and Raj frequently thanked the gods for the gift they'd presented him in the form of the goddess Sasha.

"Why did you throw her away, you idiot? Why did you do what you did?"

Raj shivered and sat upright. The trip down memory lane had dissociated him from reality. He hadn't noticed another man sitting down next to him and beginning a conversation.

"I'm sorry, what did you say?"

"I said, that's a good picture. Did you take it?"

"Oh. No, I did not."

"Who is she, if I may ask?"

"That's my ex-girlfriend. She passed away a year ago."

"I'm sorry. It must be hard for you."

"It is, periodically."

"What brings you here, to the police station, with a photo of your dead girlfriend?"

"I found a wallet on the street, I just came here to report it."

"Hey, I've also lost my wallet recently, to that god-awful pickpocket. Can you show it to me, if, by chance, it's mine?"

"Yeah, sure."

Raj took out the wallet from his pocket and showed it to the man, who said it did not belong to him. Noticing that one of the policemen was now free, he smiled goodbye at the stranger and walked up to the counter. The policeman was a young fellow by the name of Percy Weatherby.

"Have you also lost your wallet today, sir?"

"Oh, no. I'm here to deposit a wallet. A lady dropped it on the street, but before I could give it to her, I lost her in the crowd."

"Ok. When and where did this happen?"

"Just outside the Queen's Theatre, about an hour ago."

"Was there any identification in the wallet?"

"No."

"Very well, sir. Can you hand the wallet over to me?"

Raj handed it over.

"Did you steal the wallet, sir?"

"Excuse me?"

"Don't take it the wrong way, sir. I myself have just filed 37 pickpocketing cases in the last two hours, all from the same area, so when we have someone turn up here with a wallet, there is some suspicion."

"I did not steal the wallet. There's nothing in it worth stealing anyway."

The photograph in Raj's pocket felt slightly heavy as he exited the police station after depositing the wallet with the nosy police officer, who'd been overly suspicious of Raj's good intentions.

Raj was very tired, and although the trips down memory lane had roused him a little, the lethargy was returning and he found himself unable to walk the distance between the police station and the nearest tube stop. He decided to take a cab home.

Raj's usual saviour and trusted friend, Uber, deserted him this time by revealing that it would take 34 minutes for the nearest cab to arrive, due to the terrible traffic conditions. He had to wait 10 minutes before a black cab showed up and after a bit of bargaining, he was finally on his way home. Stuck in a mile-long jam a few minutes later, Raj found himself thinking about Sasha once again. A memory he had tried to delete after the heartbreak was now finding its way back into his life. Despite Raj trying to think of the world-class pizza that he would be ordering for dinner, his mind was taking him back to reminiscences of Sasha.

Their second date had been even more memorable than the first. Raj had managed to arrange a cruise on the Thames and both of them had enjoyed a lovely Saturday afternoon together, basking in the sun and feasting on food. They had hit the home run shortly after, back at Raj's house, and had officially become boyfriend and girlfriend. They simultaneously updated their relationship status on Facebook and within minutes their inbox was flooded with congratulatory messages from friends and family. It seemed as though life was perfect for Raj at that time. Success onstage and television and domestic bliss. Sasha really was the complete package. Aside from being a really beautiful woman, she was also a very successful medical practitioner, and was a very caring and kind individual. The Bonnie to his Clyde. The Pam to his Jim.

They were good together. They had the same interests. They liked the same music, loved the same films, the same food, the same brand of alcohol.

"Why?"

Movement brought Raj back to reality. Traffic had eased up, allowing the taxi to move after a long time. Raj silently prayed for no more traffic and turned his attention to the streets outside. Evening was setting in slowly, and children were coming outside their houses, some wearing football boots while others favoured the bat and ball. Mothers were chatting while pushing their babies in their prams. Two men were drunk and were fighting outside the bar. Sasha.

Suddenly, Raj's eyes widened. On the other side of the road was Sasha. He was sure it was her. She looked exactly like the photograph. Her hair, her clothes, the slight hint of lipstick. She was staring straight ahead, into the eyes of Raj, who was staring back, in shock and with his mouth open. She continued staring, before lifting her hand in the air, in the form of a wave. A car passed by. He blinked.

Sasha was not there anymore. She just wasn't there on the pavement at all. She had vanished.

"What's the matter, sir?" the taxi driver enquired, looking in the rear-view mirror to see a dishevelled Raj sweating profusely.

"It's nothing. Nothing at all. I'm just tired. Concentrate on the road, please."

Maybe his weariness, coupled with his emotions and mental state, had forced him to imagine Sasha on the pavement. Maybe it was just a trick of the light. She couldn't have been alive. Not after what he'd heard.

Entering his bachelor pad, Raj tossed his bag on the sofa, got undressed and went in to the shower. For the first seven minutes, he just stood under the hot water and allowed it to soothe the tired muscles of his body and his aching head. After going through his comprehensive post-shower routine, a now relaxed Raj enjoyed the pizza he had ordered while watching a film on Netflix.

Raj munched down the pizza in record time, such was his hunger. He put his dishes in the dishwasher, threw the box the pizza had come in into the trash bin, locked the doors, stared at the photograph once again and headed to bed.

Sleep did not come easily to Raj that night. It was an unusually warm night by London standards, and despite Raj turning on the fan and the air-conditioner, he still felt it was stuffy. If he tried to sleep, he would see Sasha's face staring back at him, the day she discovered his infidelity. Eyes near tears, hair dishevelled, anger etched on her face, as if she would just punch him, or worse.

The relationship had begun to deteriorate about a year before her death. Raj had reached the pinnacle of his success and as a result of his growing popularity and fame, he had begun to act out. Wild parties and addictions made their way into his life, and he found himself giving less and less time to Sasha. Sasha wasn't needy, she was supportive. She didn't fight with him over his late nights and early mornings, but did so when he returned home drunk and high, or didn't show up for days at a time and behaved erratically. Raj would defend himself by saying that he was a star now, and that this was acceptable and she would have to put up with it, which she refused to do. Sasha was never really able to come to terms with the way Raj changed so quickly and Raj himself became too successful too fast. He refused to mend his ways, and Sasha refused to back down. Their fights went from a monthly event, to a bi-weekly event, to a weekly haranguing, to a daily dose of argumentative discussions. In the midst of this, Raj had begun working on a production of *Othello*, where the actress playing Bianca turned out to be a big fan of his and requested some extra rehearsals from him, which was only a ruse to sleep with him, which eventually led to Sasha walking in on him and their break-up.

Raj picked up his phone to go through some of the messages that he had sent to Sasha shortly after their break-up, apologising and asking her to reconsider. Alongside each message he could see the blue tick indicating it had been read, but not a single reply from Sasha. Sleep finally came to Raj at 3 a.m., but dreams of Sasha tortured him.

A groggy Raj woke at nine the next morning and headed towards the kitchen, where he made breakfast. If you can call pouring milk over muesli making breakfast, then that is what he did. He picked up his bowl of cereal and went towards the floor-to-ceiling windows in his living room, to look at the lovely view of the city.

Munching cereal, he suddenly saw, from the corner of his eye, a woman walking in the direction of his house. He turned, saw the face of the woman and sloshed some milk over his bare feet.

It was Sasha. He wasn't mistaken. He couldn't be. It was Sasha, walking down the street, towards his house. The exact same clothing as yesterday. Raj put his cereal on a coffee table and rushed to the sink. He splashed ice cold water on his face, once, twice, three times, slapped himself a few times, made sure that he was awake, and headed back to the window.

She was still there, staring at Raj. She raised her hand in a wave. Raj could make out a slight hint of a smile playing at the corner of her mouth. Then Sasha lowered her hand and began walking away.

Raj threw on a pair of shorts and his shoes and raced out onto the street, heading in the direction where Sasha was. He'd marked a spot in his head where he would come face to face with Sasha. He reached there in good time.

Nobody. No Sasha. People were walking, catching the bus, heading to the tube station, getting on with their lives and their jobs. And Raj was hunting for a girlfriend who had been dead four months in the streets outside his house. Doctors would call that grief. Others would call it guilt, perhaps.

Raj could not understand why all of a sudden, he was seeing visions of Sasha. He had almost forgotten about her and then, suddenly, he was remembering things he did not want to remember.

The photograph.

It was the photograph.

Raj had not thought about Sasha for a long time and then he had seen the photograph which had made him go down memory lane. And then he began to think of a most strange, but viable, theory. The person who had dropped the wallet did not do so by accident. Raj felt that the person, whoever she was, wanted Raj to find the wallet and take a peek inside it. He felt as if she had something to do with him and Sasha, and was playing tricks with Raj.

Raj turned up for the rehearsal slightly later than everyone. He had once again slipped into a reverie about Sasha at the coffee shop. The first thing he noticed when he entered the theatre were two men seated in the auditorium, in the front row. An explanation was provided by Marshall.

"Got some of my friends over here for an impartial opinion of the performance. Also, we're not doing your scenes right now, so if you want, you can change and take a seat and watch as well. And if you have any feedback, you can tell us later."

Raj thought this was fine. Watching the play from a different perspective could help in identifying areas of concern people would normally miss out on. It would also offer Raj a break from thinking about Sasha, at least for an hour. Two, if they were working with the understudies. Looking forward to watching the play as audience, Raj made his way into the common green room, which was a mix of order and chaos. He, luckily, had his own room, where he could be in peace and focus on the task at hand.

His green room looked just the way he had left it the previous day. It was a large rectangular room, with a small bed at one end, and a set of sofas at another. The bathroom was right opposite the sofas. There was a large table in the centre of the room, which was piled with all sorts of unrelated garbage. A solitary chair with its back facing the door was also present. A copy of the script was on the table, with notes and ideas scribbled in the margins, and next to it was a half-full bottle of Scotch.

Raj threw his bag onto the sofa and picked up the bottle of whiskey, downing its contents in one swig. He subsequently turned his attention to the script, where he had marked the scene where Hamlet discovers Ophelia's death for practice. He still had uneven delivery while saying these lines. On his own, in his green room, he was able to nail the scene time and time again. But he faltered as soon as he was in a rehearsal. Something about Hamlet's guilt weighed on his own mind and as a result, he struggled with those lines. People thought it was emoting but he was actually suffering mildly.

Raj sat down at the table and began rehearsing. He went through the motions of the scene and focused on bringing out Hamlet's pain.

Engrossed in his lines, he suddenly became aware of a strong smell. It was a perfume, wafting in the air and into his senses.

"Who's there?" he turned around to see Anne.

"How did you get in?"

"Your door was unlocked. I knocked twice and you didn't respond so I just came inside to see if all was well."

"Nonsense. My door is always locked."

"Well, it wasn't locked this time."

"What perfume are you wearing?"

"What perfume? It's ...uh ...Calvin Klein. Mystery Woman. Why do you ask?"

"Nothing. My ex-girlfriend had a similar perfume."

"The one who died?"

"Yeah, how did you know?"

"Marshall told me. Also, the rehearsal is starting and he wants you there as soon as possible."

"Ok. Let's go."

The walk from the green room to the stage was quiet. Marshall was seated in the first row alongside his friends. He called Raj over to say the scene of the confrontation between Hamlet and Ophelia's brother, Laertes, with the understudies, would be done differently and told him to take notes, in case any change was required.

Raj sat down between Marshall's friends, introducing himself and asking politely how they were doing.

The lights of the auditorium dimmed, and after a minute, the stage was illuminated. There was a grand bed in the centre of the stage, on which Raj's understudy, Max, was sleeping. A lump on the other side of the bed indicated that there was another person alongside.

A doorbell pinged, which surprised Raj as *Hamlet* was written at a time when doorbells were not used. Max awoke and looked groggily at, to Raj's consternation, a modern alarm clock at the bedside.

Realising it was late, Max began running around, gathering clothes and tossing them inside the wardrobe while shaking the lump, asking it to get up. The doorbell continued to ring, with each ring becoming more and more aggressive. Max's face depicted a look of real urgency, as he was now pleading with the lump to awaken or else there would be "real carnage". As if on cue, the ringing stopped and Raj could hear aggressive footsteps in the wings. The curtains shook.

Out walked Sasha.

In a moment of pure fear, Raj realised what was being depicted onstage.

Sasha was staring at Max. No words were exchanged. Sasha's face was a mask of sadness. Max guiltily stared at the lump, which finally began to stir. The person emerged.

Raj's head did a backflip. Bianca.

Bianca stared drunkenly into space before she realised that someone else was in the room and, as she figured out who it was, she let out a squeal of horror and tried to stand up.

"Stay where you are" came out coldly from Sasha's mouth. She was now seething as she looked at Max.

She slapped him, once, twice, three times. Max's face grew red. Sasha said, as coldly as before, "How could you?"

She exited the stage with one final scathing look at Madhav, who was lost for words.

Darkness fell onstage.

Raj got up to leave, and found that Marshall's friends had got up as well and had formed a wall between him and freedom.

"Excuse me, gentlemen, I have to leave."

"Trust me, you don't."

Raj had not realised how intimidating these two men were until now. They were much taller than him, and very well-built. He could not possibly break through. Behind him were the green rooms. No exit there. Resigned, he sat back down as the stage was illuminated once again, this time with only Sasha standing at dead centre. She was standing with a suitcase in her hand, another puzzling addition to *Hamlet*, thought Raj until he now realised the

Shakespearean play was not being depicted onstage.

It was not *Hamlet*. It was a haranguing.

A booming voice came from somewhere:

"You're making a mistake, Sasha. Come back before it's too late."

This elicited tears in Sasha's eyes, who was staring straight into Raj's eyes.

"If you don't, there will be trouble."

"Don't leave me on seen."

"Consider this a warning, Sasha."

"Sasha???"

"This is my final warning, Sasha."

The voiceover ended abruptly.

Sasha was still staring at Raj, who had tried to turn but was drawn back time and time again to Sasha's face.

Her mouth opened.

"And what happened after that, Raj?"

Raj was dumbstruck with shock.

"What did you do, Raj?"

By this point, Raj was in tears. Sasha was staring at him, exactly as she had done when she had found out about Bianca. The pain in her voice mirrored her anguish as she had questioned him that day.

Raj recalled how, after she had broken up with him, he had become possessive. He had wanted her back at any cost. He had become threatening. He had started to become violent.

Sasha, loudly:

"WHAT DID YOU DO?"

Raj stared back at her and finally found himself speaking words he had thought he would take to the grave.

"I made a mistake. After you died, I became maniacal. I wanted you back. I did not want to say sorry, but I wanted you. I don't know why. You weren't responding. I got word that you were trying to leave the city. So, I hired a guy."

"And what happened then?"

"I asked him to get rid of you. I feared you would go to the police, or to the media, and my career would be ruined. So, I asked him to silence you."

"I asked him to kill you."

The lights went out. There was a shuffling of feet and some loud sniffles, before the entire theatre was lit.

Raj had sunk to the floor in tears.

"Get up."

He obeyed.

He looked up to see that the entire cast had joined Sasha on stage. If she was Sasha.

The shock dissipated from Raj's face. Standing onstage was Anne, holding the wig and the glasses that had transformed her into Sasha. Raj stared at her in an amalgamation of shock, horror and incredulity.

All he could utter was a series of stammers. There was no clarity, no thought. Finally, when he was able to say something, he said:

"Who're you?"

"I'm Anne. Sasha's sister. Her twin sister."

Raj's face betrayed his emotions. His eyes were open wide.

You would want to know the whole story, I know. So, let me tell you. I got the messages from Sasha. Screenshots. She was scared. She was worried you would do something. That's why she made plans to leave. I was finishing my doctoral studies and I had arranged a flat for her close to my university campus. When she died, I thought it was just a car accident. That is what the police told me. You weren't at the funeral, so I got suspicious, but my parents didn't want me to leave my studies. All I had were her messages, my suspicions, and a long period ahead to try and get you to confess."

"So, you got close to me, got to know everyone here and then started to dress as Sasha?"

"Something like that. This whole production was engineered by me. Everyone, every single cast member, was handpicked by me, to help with the plan. Even Marshall was in on it."

Raj looked at Marshall, who shrugged his shoulders.

"And let me guess, these two friends of Marshall's, they're detectives?"

"Precisely."

The jig was up. Raj had one final question.

"If you had those suspicions, why did you wait till yesterday to start tormenting me?"

"I thought that after a good performance, when you felt as if you were the king of the world, that would be the perfect time to send you into a state of shock. We also had to practise amongst ourselves. The plan to draw you in was very elaborate and we had to be very precise. And when I felt we were ready, we struck.

"Why did you do it, Raj? Sasha loved you, with all her heart. She wanted you to succeed and be the best you could be. And you killed her, Raj. Why?"

"I don't know, Anne. I don't know why I did what I did. I can't give you closure, nor can I forgive myself for what I've done. I thought I got away from it all but I should have known, Sasha was one lady you could not get away from. She'd be proud of you. The way you've brought me down."

"Take him away, officers."

One of the officers produced handcuffs and placed them around Raj's wrists, as he winced slightly. They escorted Raj out.

Inside the theatre, Anne managed a sad smile as everybody clustered around her in a silent embrace after what had been a truly magnificent performance.

HOSTAGES

"Ladies and gentlemen, there is a truly outrageous scene unfolding here today."

Turning up the volume of the news, Rohit massaged the side of his neck, where one could make out faint ligature marks. He had been experimenting with a belt today, hoping it could knock him out good for a few hours, after which he would try again and again and again, hoping to attend nirvana with his final attempt.

Sure, Rohit had tendencies. And he often caved to them, finding nothing worth living for. Rohit was a police negotiator by profession. Being a police negotiator in India is like that meme of a balcony without a window. Something unnecessary. Because here in the lovely subcontinent, dialogue, negotiation and rationality often fly out the window when the police get involved. They are mandated by law to keep a negotiator on board so that if the blue moon rises and the service of the negotiator is called upon, they are not in a sad spot.

Rohit had prepared to be a negotiator in the United States. He had trained under the great Federal Bureau of Investigation, which had a spotless record when it came to negotiating with 'hostiles. Although Rohit met the criterion for a work visa, problems back home meant that he had to ditch a blossoming career and a nice hefty pay cheque and return to his native city, Ahmedabad, where religious tensions had by then snowballed into complete carnage. His father was a Hindu and his mother were a Muslim, which meant that the radical groups in the city were going to target them first and ask them where their loyalties lay. Rohit was unable to return home on time, and although he was able to locate his mother after searching for her, he never managed to figure out the whereabouts of his father, who was presumed dead. Years later, news would arrive that Rohit's father had fled to Mumbai due to a threat on his life issued because he had been harbouring Muslims in his house during the riots. He had died in Mumbai under mysterious circumstances, and the news provider did not go into any more detail.

Rohit had moved his mother to New Delhi shortly after finding her and that is where she breathed her last, passing away in 2015.

This incident, coupled with the dull monotony of Rohit's work life and the lack of action inside his home drove him towards an unhealthy mental space. Rohit became despondent. Nihilistic. Anti-social. In 2015 alone, he had tried to jump ahead the queue four times and reach the other side, and he had been sporadically experimenting since. He had whizzed past the Pearly Gates a few times during these experiments, when he could hear the angels singing his favourite songs, and his father calling out to him, asking him to come and feast on some jalebi. He rued the fact that he had not passed through them. After his attempts were discovered by a co-worker in 2018, Rohit was asked to attend regular therapy, and reassigned to a position which was professionally more rewarding. But although he scaled back on the number of bids he made on his own life every few months, the thought never left his mind and he had been placed on temporary leave just a few days back. And so, he was in his bedroom today, where he had experimented with a belt, and had then become engrossed in a live news report that was to change his life. Only he did not know that.

Right on cue, the phone began to buzz.

***

Mattresses are the iPad of the future, said Uday Tiwari, the greatest modern thinker to emerge from the Indian subcontinent.

Uday Tiwari made mattresses. At least, his company did. And his company made the best mattresses in the world, according to a UN mattress ranker.

Uday had been born into wealth. His father was also a businessman and was involved in the olive oil business. After his father's death, Uday joined the company and worked as an olive oil producer for a few years before switching his interests to the mattress market. Realising that India did not have quality mattress producers and that most of the people used foreign produced mattresses, Uday sought to monopolize the Indian market with high quality and slightly affordable mattresses. Soon enough, Comfort+ had managed to remove all the competitors from the market to become the most popular mattress brand in India and one of the most profitable Indian companies. Over time, Comfort+ became renowned for their innovations in the mattress industry, including the introduction of a mattress for single people and India's first smart mattress, which had Alexa built into it. A mattress that could do a lot of work, including, but not limited to, tell the government what you were doing. But don't tell them I said that. They also introduced a special medical mattress, which had been touted to a lot of people suffering from bodily aches and pains.

However, all was not well.

Ever since Comfort+ became popular, Uday Tiwari began running what can only be described as a covert backdoor operation. What's that, you ask?

Well, he began selling higher quality mattresses to his rich friends for lower prices. And lower quality mattresses, most often faulty ones, were sold to the general public at higher market rates. At present, one would be able to buy a top-of-the-line normal Comfort+ mattress for INR 1,35,000. The medical mattress would set you back by 5,00,000. Add another 5,00,000 to it for the smart one. This is the price the general public was paying. And they were slowly growing dissatisfied. Mattresses were being found to be lumpy, uncomfortable, not having the advertised features, and in most cases, the advertised features not working properly. Some people began to complain that the default language of Alexa kept changing. One day she would be responding in English and then all of a sudden, you have Russian Alexa in your bedroom. Hmmm… As the complaints kept on growing, the Supreme Court of India demanded an investigation into the business practices of Comfort+, where this backdoor operation was revealed. Uday Tiwari's image was permanently tarnished when it was revealed that, for many middle-class families, the mattresses bust the bank. On the other hand, it came to the fore that Uday Tiwari had sold his mattresses for as low as 40,000 INR to his friends. As his strategies weren't illegal, just frowned upon, he couldn't be arrested.

Due to the many vagaries of the judicial system in India, and the fact that Uday held considerable sway with the government, the lawsuits that people had filed against him were taking time to come to fruition. Many were dismissed as well, and as a result, Uday Tiwari went on cheerfully with his good life. Even though he had been removed from the board of Comfort+, he continued as the chairman of his father's olive oil company and kept them in the competition. His public image had been tarnished, but his social life remained unaffected. And on that day, he had woken up with a much younger woman by his side, whom he had managed to woo at a bar the previous night. When his phone rang, he was in half a mind to carry forward the business the two of them had gotten to the previous night.

***

Adi Tiwari was not appreciated by his father. Although he succeeded both academically and as an athlete, he never managed to gain the smallest bit of affection from him. Adi never knew his mother. According to his father, she had died from 'childbirth-related complications', which a questioning and thoughtful Adi attributed as the reason for his father's continued cold shoulder towards him.

Adi worked for his father. Literally. Even though he had managed to top the all-India rankings in the national exams, his father forced him to not go to college and instead employed him as his servant. Adi was now working as his father's chauffeur/washerman/errandboy/gardener/waiter/masseuse/chef. He did everything. No vacation days. Minimum wage. The only upside, as described by his father, was that Adi continued to live in the family's luxurious estate. Even if he had gruelling days, he returned to a comfortable bed and a shower that could double up as a sauna. All that Adi wished for, was for his father to show him some love, for him to admit, just once, that he was proud of his son. If he heard that, he would find even in his life of drudgery some joy and some meaning. But he also knew that it was not going to happen until his father was alive.

On this day in the story, Adi had been sent out to run some errands. He had to pick up some groceries, followed by some medicines for his father. He was almost glad when the gunman showed up at the pharmacy and asked everyone, especially Adi, to hit the floor.

***

Dev Mittal was a low-ranked executive who worked for a mid-range paper company. His salary wasn't great, the benefits weren't so either, the hours were terrible, the bosses were evil and his wife was sick. Dev's wife had originally been a woman in perfect health, but one day she was hit by a speeding car while returning home after a walk in the park. The impact and subsequent fall left her with a spinal injury. She would have trouble walking, sleeping and performing ordinary tasks, and also became prone to suffering long and intense bouts of pain. With limited financial resources at their disposal, the Mittal's ran pillar to post to search for help. The public healthcare system was poor and private healthcare prohibitive. The couple took loans and consulted several professionals until it stumbled upon the medical mattress of Comfort+. Despite the exorbitant price, the Mittal's went ahead with the purchase, in the hope that it would help Mrs Mittal out if only a little bit.

Sadly, that outcome never materialised.

Due to Mattressgate, the Mittal's ended up with a poor-quality medical mattress. Owing to its shoddy craftsmanship and missing features, Mrs Mittal's back problems got exacerbated until they reached a point where she was now unable to move and had become bedridden. This drove Dev mad, as he couldn't bear to see her like that. He wanted his beloved wife to be on her feet again, but with his limited resources, he knew it would take a while. And so, he came up with a plan. He decided to take Adi Tiwari hostage, in the hopes that he could extract a ransom from Uday Tiwari, which he would use to treat his wife at the best international hospitals.

Dev began doing covert surveillance of Adi Tiwari and quickly realised that he was alone for many hours a day. It would make it easy for Dev to kidnap him. Dev, however, did not want to kidnap Adi and take him away as he knew that it would not be viable. He wanted to publicly show Uday Tiwari what his actions had led to and why Dev was doing what he was doing. Which is why he planning a hostage scene.

After observing him, Dev realised that Adi made regular trips to the pharmacy. The pharmacy had minimal protection and could, at certain points during the day, hold a lot of people, making it the ideal location for Dev to sneak in and hold the customers hostage at the point of a weapon. He purchased a few guns from the black market, including a Mauser rifle, Walther, Glock and Colt handguns, and stopped showing up at work until it was D-Day.

***

"Are you watching the news, Rohit," came the voice over the phone. It belonged to his supervisor.

"Yes, sir," said Rohit.

"I want you ready and headed towards the spot right now. As far as we know, there are 12 civilians inside the pharmacy, including Adi Tiwari, who is priority #1," said the boss.

"What are his demands?"

"He wants 80 lakhs in cash from Uday Tiwari in the next three hours and he wants immunity until his wife is treated, which, unfortunately, we cannot give him. If he doesn't get the money, he is going to become hostile. Right now, he is treating his hostages well, but he has suggested force should Uday Tiwari refuse to pay up."

"Have you gotten in touch with Mr Tiwari?"

"We have not been able to get in touch with him just yet. I'm going to send you the contact details we have and I want you to start negotiating with him and the hostile as soon as you get there. We cannot afford to lose civilians. Not today." It was election week.

"Have I made myself clear?"

"Sir, yes sir."

With that, Rohit cut the call. threw on his uniform and rushed out towards the pharmacy. He arrived at the pharmacy in 10 minutes and was greeted by his deputy, Rakesh. There was a horde of cameras and reporters asking for the dope.

"Talk to me, Rakesh. What's the scene," Rohit asked.

"We've got 12 civilians, including the hostile, inside the pharmacy. The hostile is armed. So far, we know he's got a local revolver, but there is a bag present with him inside where we think there could be more arms and ammunition. We've got men stationed at every possible exit to the building. We've got a sniper over there should the situation get out of control. Do you know his demands?"

"Yeah. 80 lakhs INR in cash. But not just that. He wants Uday Tiwari to personally come and deliver the money. He wants to speak to him face-to-face."

"Dear Lord. Any info about who he is, the hostile?"

"He is apparently a man by the name of Dev Mittal. Works for our local paper company."

"Why, then, is a paper salesman holding the son of a mattress tycoon hostage inside a goddamn pharmacy?"

"We don't know. We were hoping you could figure it out."

"Anybody got in touch with Tiwari Sr. yet?"

"No. Not yet."

"Get on the phone, now."

Rakesh hurried away, dialling a number on his mobile phone.

Rohit picked up the megaphone and moved towards the entry to the pharmacy.

"Dev, can you hear me?"

Silence, which was followed by a low voice responding in the affirmative.

"Dev, I'm Rohit. I'm the negotiator. Can you tell me why you're doing this?

Silence again.

Then... "Where's that son of a gun Uday Tiwari?"

"We're trying to get in touch with him, Dev. But till then, my job is to understand why you're doing what you're doing and ensure no lives are lost.

"I don't want to kill anybody. I just want the money."

"If you can tell me why you are after the money, it will make everything easier."

"That man sold me a fake mattress. I wanted a good mattress so that my wife, who has back problems, could feel better. Because of the faulty mattress, she is now bedridden. Unable to move. I don't have money to take care of her."

"And so, you're holding his son hostage."

***

"I want him to see what he's done... to the people of his country. He needs a wake-up call. Maybe, his son's life being at risk, that would be a big one."

Inside the pharmacy, Adi was gesturing frantically towards Dev.

"Hold on, officer. I'll be back with you shortly."

"Wait, Dev, please."

"What do you want, Tiwari?

"Listen, man. I think you're mistaken."

"You're not Adi Tiwari?"

"Oh yes, I am. I'm not going to deny that. The thing is, my father has no affection for me. So, he would not be very willing to pay the money to you, unless something drastic happens, you know. Like you fire some shots or something. Because he is not going to pay you a single rupee if you just keep talking like that."

And it was true.

Rakesh, too, had managed to get through to Uday Tiwari, and then the conversation had borne the same outcome.

"Who's this?"

"Mr Tiwari, this is Rakesh Gupta from the Delhi Police. Do you know why I'm calling you?"

"Let me guess, my son's been arrested for a DUI? Speeding? How much is the fine?"

"No sir. It's not about that. Your son is being held hostage at the A1 Pharmacy."

"What?"

"Yes sir. A man by the name of Dev Mittal has held your son and 10 other civilians' hostage inside the pharmacy and he is demanding 80 lakhs in cash from you."

"Not happening."

"Excuse me?"

"You heard me right the first time, officer. I am not going to do that."

"This is your son we're talking about, Mr Tiwari. It's important that we co-operate and negotiate with the hostile."

"He is not my son. Never was. And I am not going to negotiate. Goodbye."

With that he cut the call.

"Who was that?" the girl on Uday's bed began to enquire.

"Nobody."

"Sounded pretty intense."

"Nothing you need to worry about. Now, where were we?"

"That sounded serious, Uday. Who was it?"

"Nothing. Just the small matter of my son being held hostage at a pharmacy."

"What?"

"Yeah. Nothing major."

"Nothing major?"

"Yeah."

"Your son is held hostage inside a pharmacy. He might die, and you want to make love over here."

"Yes."

"Are you insane?"

"No."

"This is your son. Your flesh and blood."

"He is not my son."

Uday Tiwari had lied to Adi. Or, in polite language, deceived him. Adi's mother had not died at childbirth. The truth was far more complicated. Back in his heydays, Uday had had numerous affairs, and at one point in time slept with a different woman every night. One of these women was Adi's mother. Unbeknownst to him, she had become pregnant and had given birth to Adi without informing Uday. When Adi was two, a terrible illness befell her and she passed away, leaving Adi in the care of his father. Uday refused to accept Adi as a son, deeming him illegitimate. He provided for his education, ensured he remained healthy, but aside from that, couldn't really give two hoots about Adi, which is why he made him work practically like his servant.

"So, you see, Sheila, he is not my son. Just a liability put on my shoulders at a time I didn't need one. His arrival ruined my life, Sheila."

"So, you're going to let him die, just because he arrived unexpectedly at your doorstep one day and you had to take care of him?"

"Since when did *you* become the voice of rationality?"

"You are insufferable. You really are. I don't know why I became friends with you of all people. I have never met a more heartless man in my life. Shame on you."

Sheila grabbed her things in a fit of rage, slapped Uday Tiwari across the face a few times, screamed at him to wake up, come to his senses and mend his ways around Adi, and left. A stunned Uday Tiwari remained seated on his bed.

Back at the pharmacy, Rakesh had just informed Rohit about Uday Tiwari's unwillingness to negotiate.

"My word, that man. Does he not realize his son's life is in danger?"

"Evidently he doesn't."

"Well, Dev hasn't posed a threat yet, but we can't let him know that Uday Tiwari is not willing to negotiate. Because he could turn hostile really quickly. We have to stall him and negotiate with Mr Tiwari. There has to be some way."

As if on cue, a bullet emerged through the glass window of the pharmacy and lodged itself into the wall of a building on the opposite side of the road, sending a large group of onlookers into a tizzy, for Dev had just turned hostile.

Rohit rushed forward, grabbing the microphone.

"Hey, Dev. What are you doing?"

"I heard Tiwari Sr was unwilling to pay."

"What?"

"His son told me. Apparently, Tiwari Sr doesn't love his son at all."

"How can you be sure?"

"I don't think his son would lie at a time like this. Is Tiwari going to pay?"

"We haven't had the chance to completely get that sorted with Mr Tiwari, Dev. So, we really can't say."

"He has two hours. Tell him that."

With that, Dev went away from the door, back towards the hostages, leaving Rohit standing outside, nonplussed.

The negotiations were getting complicated, now that Adi Tiwari had, from inside the pharmacy, influenced Dev.

"What do we do, Rakesh," Rohit said.

"Storm the building, as we do every time," Rakesh suggested.

"That's a very risky move. If we storm it, he might get even more hostile and fire back. He could kill some people inside as well. We have to be calm", was Rohit's response.

"But Tiwari is unwilling to negotiate. He said as much."

"If he is not going to negotiate, we will make him negotiate."

Suddenly, Rohit experienced an epiphany. An epiphany that could change the fortunes of everyone present there. He called his superiors and informed them of his plan. They were initially sceptical, but Rohit accepted full responsibility should his plan go wrong, and they agreed to it.

Rohit walked up to the news vans, of which only three were remaining, as the others had left due to budgetary reasons. He offered them the opportunity of getting a first-hand look at what was happening inside the pharmacy, which they lapped up eagerly. Rohit then walked to the entrance of the pharmacy and rapped his fingers on the door, asking for Dev's attention.

"Who is it?" came Dev's voice from inside.

"It's me again," said Rohit.

"What do you want? Is Tiwari Sr. negotiating."

"I have a plan, but I need your help."

"Why do I help you?"

"You help me, you help yourself."

There was a pause. Then Dev spoke, tentatively.

"Do you even know whether the plan is going to work?"

"What did Adi tell you? Why did you fire the bullets?"

"He said that, if we were to get money out of Uday, then we had to shock him into acceptance. We had to show him what his actions had led to, not just tell."

"Precisely. Till now, he hasn't seen for himself what's happened. And I want to make him see."

"What are you implying?"

"I want to bring the reporters inside. I want them to show the reality of the situation to the whole city, to the whole country, to the whole world if need be. That should be a big enough shock for Mr Tiwari, don't you think so?"

"Why would I do this for you?"

"Normally, I wouldn't do this either, but these are strange circumstances and you are not the most conventional hostage taker. And like I said, you help me, you help yourself."

"What do you want me to do?"

Rohit gave him some instructions. He basically set-up a hostage situation, within a hostage situation. The reporters had phoned back to their stations which were readying the newscasters and the teleprompter. Tweets regarding an impending change in the hostage situation had begun doing the rounds, and the whole country was at a standstill, glued to their television screens, as the countdown towards the biggest news story-cum-crime drama of the year began.

Rohit dialled Uday Tiwari's number.

"Hello. Who is this?"

"Hello, Mr Tiwari, I am Rohit, the police negotiator involved with your son's case."

"I told you guys, I am not negotiating."

"And I know that, sir. What my colleague failed to inform you was that you then had two hours to meet the hostage taker's demands. If you don't do that, he is going to turn hostile. He has already fired three shots, and is slowly getting concerned by your inaction. As of this moment, you have an hour and 10 minutes to meet his demands, or he kills your son. If you don't want your son to die, I suggest that you tune into one of our country's three major news channels within the next 10 minutes. Maybe that would change your mind. If not, you can start preparing for your son's funeral proceedings after the clock strikes 2. Thank you."

Rohit disconnected the phone line and began readying everybody around the pharmacy for one of the most unconventional negotiation moves the world would ever see. The FBI would be proud.

The clock struck 1.

Uday switched on the television. Onscreen, the news anchor spoke excitedly.

"Ladies and gentlemen. What we have here today is something that has never happened before. We are going to provide you with a first-hand account of the A1 Pharmacy hostage situation. Our camera crews are going to show you what is actually taking place over here, inside the pharmacy, in the hopes that we, as a nation, are able to put pressure on the required parties to end the hostage situation. We now go to

Mr Rohit, the lead negotiator on the case, who is the mastermind behind this operation."

"Yes, thank you, sir," a tall, smartly dressed man in a blue shirt and a negotiator, with a shock of black hair and a lean face, came onto the screen and spoke into the reporter's hand. He said:

Ladies and gentlemen of this country, this is a strange moment. As most of you know, we have a hostage situation with us. And as most of you know, the person being held hostage is the son of one of our country's biggest businessmen. A businessman, who is unwilling to pay the abductor what he wants. A businessman who wants to throw away the life of his son. His life is not worth losing. Nobody's is. We shouldn't be in a situation moping for loss of life if we have a situation so easily preventable."

Twitter was already going wild. The hashtags #SaveAdiTiwari and #WakeUpUdayTiwari were already breaking the Web. Uday was staring at the television screen in horror.

"What we are going to show you today is the reality of the situation. No sliding over topics. No hiding the truth. Exactly what is happening inside, in the hopes that, maybe, we can save these lives. The assailant is a man just like you and I. A common man. All he wanted to do was something that could help his wife with her chronic pain and disability. But the mattress he chose to accomplish the job was, sadly, below par. Hence we are where we are."

Rohit started moving forward and three videographers followed him. Rohit opened the door of the pharmacy, and the camerapersons looked inside. The whole country sat transfixed, staring at their television screens in horror, just like Uday. Dev Mittal had his gun pointed at Adi's head who was begging for mercy and pleading for his father to oblige him. The word 'please' mouthed by the boy with his face full of tears had a profound effect on those among the audience that had a heart.

Uday Tiwari had just managed to discover his own conscience. Or so it would seem to all. In the meanwhile, his phone had vibrated itself off the table, with tweets and messages from all over the world flooding in. He rapidly got up.

At the pharmacy, Rohit was wrapping up the TV report.

"Mr Tiwari, if you saw that, have a heart. Do what is required. To the public, you now know the whole story. But please, don't dehumanise our assailant. He is an ordinary man, who had to take an extraordinary step. Do not shame him. Thank you for your time."

Uday Tiwari was busy dialling his banker.

"Hello, Mr Tiwari. Did you see the news?"

"Yes, I did. That is why I am calling you. I want the 80,00,000 INR taken from my account and placed into briefcases that I will be collecting in 10 minutes. I want it done as soon as possible. No if's or but's."

He also called Rohit.

"I am on my way. Tell the guy I am on my way with the money."

Soon enough, Uday Tiwari arrived at the scene, with two briefcases filled to the rim with banknotes, where he was greeted with a horde of reporters clamouring in his face. The cameras flashed to show the world that Uday Tiwari had arrived.

The money changed hands. As Adi emerged from the pharmacy, he ran towards Uday, who embraced him, broke down in tears and apologized for his actions over the last 19 years. Dev was arrested almost immediately, but before leaving, Uday managed to get Dev's address and promised him that his wife would get the money and he would post his bail and fight the case for him, if necessary.

Take it as you will, but Uday Tiwari had had his lesson, or his awakening.

In the coming days, Uday Tiwari issued a formal apology to his customers through the media due to the events of the previous days as well as his "terrible decision-making, both personally and professionally". The events had shaken him to his core, finally giving life to a once cold heart. He provided reimbursements, partly from his own pocket and partly from the resources of the company, and also gave every family a free, high quality mattress aside from this sum. He asked his son to begin his applications for college. Adi ended up going to Harvard on a full scholarship.

Dev Mittal was released on bail shortly after his arrest and his case was assigned to a fast-track court, where he was sentenced to a six-month term of rigorous imprisonment. In the meanwhile, Uday Tiwari ensured that Mrs Mittal was sent to the best medical institutions in the world for treatment, which he was funding from his own pocket. She recovered.

Rohit was awarded multiple medals by the Indian government for his effort. He was awarded a wage hike and a promotion, and for the first time in over four years, did not feel the need to take the extreme step, to end it all, a thought that so far kept bearing down on the back of his mind. Rohit was free at long last.